FIRESTORM!

"Move, Frank, move!" Nancy shouted.

Thick, dark smoke was filling every corner of the warehouse, causing Nancy and the Hardys to cough and choke. Waves of flame tore across the floor, gliding along the sea of spilled fuel, igniting everything within the tinderbox of a building.

"Wait," Nancy cried. Pointing below, she shouted to the others, "It's no use going back the way we came. We can't go down the ladder."

"You're right," Frank answered. "The whole floor is already covered in fire!"

"What can we do?" Joe asked. Covering his mouth with his sleeve, desperately trying to keep the rising smoke out of his lungs, he added, "We're trapped."

Nancy Drew & Hardy Boys SuperMysteries

A NANCY DREW AND HARDY BOYS

SUPER MYSTERY™

PROCESS OF ELIMINATION

Carolyn Keene

AN ARCHWAY PAPERBACK
Published by POCKET BOOKS
New York   London   Toronto   Sydney   Tokyo   Singapore

AN ARCHWAY PAPERBACK *Original*

An Archway Paperback published by
POCKET BOOKS, a division of Simon & Schuster Inc.
1230 Avenue of the Americas, New York, NY 10020

Copyright © 1998 by Simon & Schuster Inc.
Produced by Mega-Books, Inc.

ISBN: 0-671-00739-4

First Archway Paperback printing April 1998

10 9 8 7 6 5 4 3 2 1

Cover art by Franco Accornero

Printed in the U.S.A.

IL 6+

PROCESS OF
ELIMINATION

Chapter

One

I WONDER WHAT could be keeping him," Nancy Drew said as she checked her watch for the tenth time in thirty minutes. She and her friends Bess Marvin and Anthony Green had been waiting for Carl Dubchek to arrive for lunch, and Nancy was beginning to worry. The lawyer and retired professor had been so precise about the address of the restaurant and the meeting time that Nancy thought it odd that he was late and hadn't called.

Now that the environmental conference was over, Nancy wasn't sure what could have caused him to be so late. She knew that Los Angeles was famous for its traffic jams. Perhaps the sudden turn in the weather had delayed him, she thought.

Outside the glass wall of windows, the rain continued to pour out of the Los Angeles sky. Far away in the hills behind the restaurant, lightning flashed against the distant cliffs. The sky grew even darker. Thunder echoed faintly a few seconds later, threatening to move closer.

"Will that be all, then?" the waiter asked the group.

"I think so," Anthony answered. He turned to Nancy and Bess. "Is everything okay with you?" he asked.

Anthony was well-built, with light brown hair and green eyes. Nancy had to admit that Bess had found herself an attractive escort while they were in California.

Bess Marvin ran a hand through her blond hair and looked at Anthony. "I suppose this will do. What do you think, Nancy?"

Nancy nodded, holding her mouth closed tight to keep from smiling. She knew Bess was trying hard to impress Anthony and so she didn't want to ruin her friend's chances.

Maybe she *does* fall in and out of love a bit too easily, Nancy thought, but she is one of my two best friends.

"Everything seems fine to me," Nancy said. "I'd like some more iced tea, though."

The waiter nodded, then hurried away.

Just then a low buzzing noise cut the air. Anthony reached under the table. As he did, the buzzing stopped. Pulling his beeper free from his belt, he held it up to read the numbers.

"Looks like I'll have to go find a phone," he said.

Anthony hesitated as he stood up. It was clear to Nancy that he didn't want to leave the table. Nancy wondered if his mood had anything to do with whoever had just beeped him. She knew Bess was hoping it had more to do with his having to leave her side.

"Is it Mr. Dubchek?" Bess asked.

"I'm not sure," Anthony answered. Then, keeping his eyes lowered, he added, "I mean, I don't recognize the number."

Nancy frowned, suspicion flashing across her blue eyes. She had the feeling that Anthony had just lied to them.

"If you'll excuse me . . ." Anthony said.

"We'll manage somehow," Bess told him. As soon as Anthony was out of earshot, she turned to Nancy. "Isn't he wonderful?"

"He's very nice," Nancy said. "But—"

"But what?" Bess asked quickly. "Is he too old? He's maybe four years older than we are. Does he live too far away? Or is it that I don't know anything about him except that he's handsome and charming? Well, which is it, Nance?"

"I was only going to ask you, but what about Arthur Truman? I thought you two were going together?"

"Oh, that was ages ago," Bess said with a shrug.

"To the best of my knowledge, that was last week," Nancy said with a chuckle.

"Don't rub it in," Bess answered, making a face at her friend.

"Hey, *you're* the one who brought up all the bad points in this relationship of yours," Nancy shot back with a grin. She slid a few strands of reddish blond hair behind her right ear. "When we were voted to represent our environmental club at this conference, I only thought about the lectures we'd be attending and getting through the speech we had to give."

"'How You Can Make Your Community More *Re*cycling *Re*sponsible,'" Bess said, reciting the title of their speech in a voice that sounded like that of a network news anchor. "Well, of course they voted for us—and George—we did get half the businesses in River Heights recycling. It's too bad George couldn't come with us."

Bess was referring to her cousin, George Fayne. George was the opposite of Bess in looks and in temperament. While Bess preferred to sit on the sidelines of most activities, George leaped in without fear. She had short, curly dark hair and dark eyes and stood several inches taller than Bess. The two were so different in so many ways that the fact that they were cousins—and best friends—surprised most people.

"Yes, I wish George could have come, too," Nancy said, "but the club had the budget to send only two people. And besides, she wasn't about to miss the soccer playoffs if she could help it. She'd practiced too long and hard not to be with her team when they play their final game tomorrow."

"I almost wish she had come instead of me," Bess said. "I mean, I'm glad I met Anthony. He's warm and sweet and funny, and I've had a really great time with him, but—"

"But what?" Nancy asked gently.

"But what am I supposed to do now? Today is the last day of the conference. Tomorrow's a free day and then Sunday we fly home. I don't know if I'll ever see him again."

"Just how serious are you two getting?" Nancy asked playfully. She watched Bess's face light up as she answered.

"Oh, Nancy—I really like him a lot. That's why I don't know what to do. What if we go home and he forgets all about me?"

Nancy drained the last of the iced tea from her glass. "I don't think he'll forget you."

Bess's face lit up mischievously. "Just to make sure he doesn't, I'll be positively fascinating until we leave. I'll tell him a different story every day until he falls hopelessly under my spell."

"Okay," Nancy said. "And just what will you tell him stories about?"

"You," Bess said. "Nancy Drew—the famous teen detective from River Heights."

"What?" The laughter that Nancy had been holding back earlier burst out of her. " 'Teen detective'? Where did you get that?"

"Well," Bess answered, trying to control her own laughter, "that *is* what they call you in the newspapers. And you have to admit that every time you turn around you *do* end up the center of attention with someone being murdered or kidnapped or blackmailed or something. . . ."

Nancy was just about to answer her friend when lightning bathed the room in a white glow and a clap of thunder sounded so loudly that it moved things on several of the tables. As the rain began to fall harder in response, making a racket against the windows, Nancy spoke louder so Bess could hear her.

"Now who's rubbing it in?"

"Sorry," Bess said. "I couldn't resist."

Nancy was about to answer when the waiter

returned with the iced tea pitcher. He filled Nancy's glass and then went off toward a well-dressed woman who was signaling frantically from across the dining room.

Alone once more, Nancy and Bess were just about to go back to their conversation when the cloudburst ended. The rain stopped so dramatically that Nancy noticed that the mood of the entire restaurant had brightened.

It seemed that all the patrons in the restaurant turned in their seats, staring at the returning sun. At two different tables, people began to applaud. The clapping was infectious, and soon everyone in the restaurant was applauding, including the wait staff.

Nancy and Bess joined in the applause. "I guess it's been raining a little too long for everybody."

"Californians," Bess said, "they don't know about anything but sunshine."

"And the occasional earthquake," Nancy added.

"I guess," Bess agreed, smiling once more. As the applause died down, Bess picked up her water glass and held it over the center of the table.

"A toast," she said. "To my friend, Nancy Drew, renowned detective. May we always be friends."

"Hear, hear," Nancy said. She picked up her

iced tea and tapped her glass against her friend's.

Looking out the window as she took a long sip, Nancy smiled to see the cloud cover burning off. Beams of sunlight began to cut through the gray sky. Maybe this is an omen, Nancy thought. Maybe everything will work out okay for Bess and Anthony.

And then, as if in response to her thought, Nancy spotted Anthony Green heading back to the table. "Here he comes now," Nancy said.

Both girls giggled, but Anthony didn't seem to notice. Nancy could tell from the look on his face that he had too much on his mind.

Anthony sat down at the table looking as if he was in a state of shock. He appeared so numb, Nancy was certain that if Bess hadn't spoken to him, he might not have noticed them at all.

"Tony," Bess asked. "What's wrong?"

"Well, I-I've been a bit concerned . . . what with Mr. Dubchek not showing up and all. I had left messages, asking people to call. . . ."

Anthony's voice trailed off. Suddenly a dark feeling formed in the pit of Nancy's stomach. "Anthony, what happened to Mr. Dubchek?" she asked.

"I can hardly say it," Anthony said. "He was shot. They don't know what happened—only that someone shot him. . . ." His voice trailed off.

"And?" Nancy asked. "Is he okay? Was he seriously hurt?"

"Yes, he was very seriously hurt." Anthony's voice cracked with emotion.

Neither Nancy or Bess was prepared for what Anthony said next.

"They killed him. He's dead!"

Chapter

Two

NANCY STARED in disbelief at Anthony. He was shaken, unable to move, unable to speak. Delivering his news seemed to have paralyzed him.

"Anthony," Nancy asked gently, "how do you know Mr. Dubchek is dead? Who told you?"

"The call I got . . . on my beeper," Anthony said in a strained voice, "it was one of the other coordinators from the conference. You know her—Mrs. Grunderson. She . . . when the police called the conference, she got the message. After they talked to her, Mrs. Grunderson thought she should call me. We were co-

coordinators, after all. Mr. Dubchek and myself, I mean . . ."

"We know," Bess said softly.

Nancy could tell by the way Anthony kept staring and from the way he was speaking that he could go into shock. "Tony," she asked slowly and clearly, "what did the police tell Mrs. Grunderson? What happened to Mr. Dubchek?"

"He died."

"We know he died, Anthony," Nancy answered. "If I heard you correctly, you said Mr. Dubchek had been shot. Was that what you said?" she asked.

"They made it sound . . . she made it sound, I mean, I didn't talk to the police, only Mrs. Grunderson—"

"Right. We know. And that's okay, Anthony," Nancy said. "But, please, answer the question. What happened to Mr. Dubchek?"

Anthony stared past Nancy and Bess. "I feel so stupid," he said.

"Why?" Nancy asked. "Tell us what's the matter, Anthony."

"I didn't think, I mean . . ."

Anthony stopped talking then. After a moment he reached for his glass. His hand shook so badly he spilled water over the side of the glass and onto the table. He set the glass back down quickly, muttering an apology.

"Take a deep breath," Bess told him.

After several deep breaths, Anthony picked up his water glass again. This time he managed to get it to his lips, drink, and then set it back down without spilling any. He seemed to be calmer.

"Sorry I fell apart there," Anthony said. "I'm okay now."

Anthony Green did not look okay to Nancy. She didn't know if he was simply nervous, or if there was something more to it. Nancy's instincts told her that Anthony was hiding something important from them.

Before Nancy could give any more thought to why Anthony was being so vague about the death of his fellow conference coordinator, the waiter returned with their lunch orders.

Once the waiter had gone back to the kitchen, Bess asked, "Tony, do you feel okay?"

"Yeah—yes. I mean, I'm fine." Nancy noticed that Anthony did not look at her or Bess but simply stared at the table. "Maybe we should just try to eat our lunches, I mean . . . since they're here and all," he said.

The three picked at their food. Nancy thought about the irony of their situation. Earlier, when it had been dark and rainy, she, Bess, and Anthony had been happy and having a good time. Now the rain had disappeared and the sun was out, but they felt miserable.

"I don't know about you two," Nancy offered, "but I don't think any of us feels much like eating anymore."

"Maybe we should go back to the conference site," Bess offered. "We could find out what happened. It might make you feel better, Tony."

Anthony's head jerked slightly. Nancy's eyes narrowed as she wondered what could have upset him—even slightly—about Bess's suggestion.

Every time I ask him anything, she thought, he ducks the question. Something tells me I'll learn a lot more by waiting to see what he does next than by pushing him to answer more questions.

Anthony didn't make her wait long.

"This is silly," he said. "What's happened is bad enough, but I'm making it worse. It's just because I feel that if he hadn't been coming here to meet us, nothing would have happened to him."

"Do you really think that?" Bess asked.

"I don't know," Anthony answered. "That's the problem. We don't know what's happened. But if I would have asked Mrs. Grunderson a few questions, I'm sure I could have found out a lot more."

13

Anthony took his napkin from his lap and set it next to his plate. "I'm going to call the police to see if I can find out anything else," he said as he stood up. "You stay here and try to enjoy your lunch. After all, no matter what's happened, we can't do anything about it by ruining the rest of our afternoon, right?"

The girls agreed, and Anthony went off to the phones once more. "He's right," Bess said, spearing a forkful of salad. "We should try to finish our lunches."

After letting a moment pass, Nancy told her friend, "You know, I do think I'm feeling hungry again. Watch my purse, will you? I'm going to sneak a look at the dessert case. I'll be right back."

"Let me know if they have any chocolate mousse," Bess asked. "Or strawberry parfaits. Or German chocolate—"

"Don't worry, I know all your favorites," Nancy said. In a few seconds she found the phone bank near the entrance to the kitchen. Spotting Anthony, she moved as close to him as she dared. From the way he was swinging his free arm to gesture, Nancy could tell that he was extremely upset.

"Listen," Nancy heard him say, "I've already talked to the police—they tracked me down here at the restaurant, and *they* told me he was dead at least fifteen minutes ago. And they told me how he died, so don't lie to me now."

Nancy's eyes narrowed as she listened to Anthony. He seemed totally absorbed with his call. Nancy decided to risk moving closer so that she could hear more.

"No way!" Anthony raised his voice unexpectedly. Nancy wondered what the person on the other end of the phone had said to anger him so much.

"No—I don't want to. No, I don't think you *can* make me."

Nancy desperately wished she could hear the other end of the conversation. She was grateful for the stylish partitions separating the phone stalls. As distracted as Anthony was, Nancy was certain she could remain unnoticed in the booth next to his.

"Listen to me, Cinder, that was before. Things are different now," Anthony was saying.

Nancy stared at the decorative wall between the two phone booths in frustration, wishing she could hear more, wishing she had some idea of what was going on. This version of his story was so different from what he'd told her and Bess.

"No, I told the police I didn't know any-

thing. And I don't—do I? Do I know anything?" Anthony paused for a moment, then
growled into the phone, "Well, maybe I did,
but I don't now. I just got amnesia, and that's
the way it's going to stay. So just forget it.
Forget all of it!"

Realizing from his last words that he was
about to hang up, Nancy dodged away from the
phones and stepped on the other side of a large
potted plant just in time. Anthony left the
phone area without noticing her.

Nancy hurried back to the table. Is Tony
directly involved with Mr. Dubchek's death?
she wondered. Did he know it was going to
happen? Was Mr. Dubchek involved with
something illegal? Was Tony? she thought with
a sinking heart.

Nancy stopped to look at the dessert display
on her way back to the table, suddenly confused
over what to do. She could question Anthony,
but what if he didn't tell her anything? What
could she do then? Go to the police? With
what? What did she know—what did she even
suspect?

For once in her life Nancy Drew simply did
not know her options. But as she drew near the
table and saw Anthony and Bess with their
heads together, a terrible feeling tore through
her. One of her best friends was falling for

someone who Nancy was afraid might be an accomplice to murder—if not worse.

Nancy smiled as she approached the table, trying not to arouse either Bess's or Anthony's suspicions. She knew she was going to have to decide on a course of action soon.

Very soon, Nancy thought grimly. Before Bess got more deeply involved with Anthony. Or before someone else got murdered.

Chapter
Three

M AN, NOW *THIS* IS HOW to spend a four-day weekend!"

Joe Hardy slapped his brother, Frank, on the back. Pointing in the direction of the monkey habitat, he added, "With sights like that, I heartily agree."

"I'm glad to hear it," Frank Hardy answered. "To tell the truth, I wasn't sure you were as interested as I was in coming to the San Diego Zoo."

The brothers had come to California with their father while the senior Hardy attended a security enforcement conference taking place over the holiday weekend. The trip was business for Mr. Hardy, a former New York City police officer who had gone on to become a well-known private detective. For the boys, it was purely a vacation—one earned by acing their latest round of exams. While their father attended a day of lectures, Joe and Frank headed for the city's famed zoo.

As Joe continued to stare in the direction of the monkeys, Frank told his brother, "You know, the San Diego Zoo was one of the first in the world to eliminate cages and create natural habitats for the animals."

"What kinds of habitats?" Joe asked.

Not understanding what his brother meant, Frank pointed in the same direction Joe had previously. "What do you mean, 'what kind?' *That* kind, right over there. You do remember that exhibit of monkeys that *you* pointed at just a moment ago, don't you?"

Joe smiled and reached up, grabbing the back of Frank's head. Turning it slightly, he aimed it at an attractive blond girl standing just a few feet to the left of the monkey's domain.

"That's what I was pointing at. With sights like that, I can leave Bayport behind any time."

"Oh, yeah?" Frank asked, raising his eyebrows. "And what about Vanessa? I thought you two were a done deal."

"Hey," Joe answered, "you're the big bad one who's got himself a steady girlfriend. Vanessa and I are friends."

Frank smiled, but let his brother's comment pass for the moment. He knew Joe liked to look at every pretty girl who came into view. He also knew that his brother could not stop thinking about a certain girl back home in Bayport.

Unable to resist teasing Joe just a bit, Frank said, "It's all right, I understand. You're my baby brother. You're allowed to be immature. Someday, though, you'll be as old as I am now. Then all will be made clear to you."

"Man, oh man." Joe laughed. He threw a fake punch at his brother. "And I thought it smelled bad near the elephants."

"Hey," Frank responded, easily dodging Joe's punch, then throwing one of his own. "You'd better watch yourself. Don't start any wars you can't finish."

"I can't believe it," Joe answered in an exaggerated drawl. "My big brother threatening me with violence. Well, now you've gone and hurt my feelings."

"And we can't have that, can we?" Frank said. "Tell you what, why don't I spring for a couple of hot dogs and we'll call it even?"

"Okay this time," Joe said. "But you watch your step," he added in a mock-stern tone.

As the two brothers walked across the open area between the monkey habitat and the nearest snack area, Frank put an arm across his brother's shoulders. "I don't know, Joe," he said. "Sometimes I wonder when you'll be summoned back to your home planet."

"Hey," Joe answered lightly as he and Frank took their places at the back of the line for the snack bar, "tell it to someone who cares."

Joe and Frank's turn came in just a few minutes. Both brothers ordered hot dogs with side orders of crinkle-cut fries and large colas. Joe got an order of onion rings and a corn dog as well.

"Did you leave anything for the lunch crowd?" Frank asked as he and Joe made their way to a bench across from the snack bar.

"Hey, I'm still growing," Joe answered. Lifting his hot dog, he slid an onion ring around the end of the frankfurter, then put the dog back down in its bun. Biting off the end, he spoke around his mouthful. "Besides, Mom says I need more nourishment."

Frank shook his head and tore into his own meal. He started on his fries, washing down the first few with a long drink of soda.

Frank ate slowly. He was in no hurry to leave the spot he and Joe had found. The sun had begun to get hotter, and he was glad they had managed to get seats in the shade. Frank mopped his brow with a napkin, thinking that the intense heat of the southern California afternoon was just a little too warm for a guy from Bayport.

As he polished off the last bite of his hot dog, Frank asked his brother, "Joe, do you ever think about going into detective work full-time when we get older?"

"Sometimes," Joe answered. "Why?"

"I don't know," Frank replied. "Maybe it's because we have free time on our hands right now. I mean we came out here while Dad did his thing. He's here working, but we're freeloading on this trip just so we can hang out."

"Hey," Joe reminded his brother, "we earned this—remember?" He popped another onion ring in his mouth. "How can you have any problem with that? I don't know too many people who would be upset with a free California vacation."

Frank shook his head. "Make no mistake. I am definitely not upset about this vacation. In fact, I think I could sit on this bench all day."

"I hear you," Joe answered. "But if we don't get up soon, we won't get to see anything else."

"I guess you're right," Frank said. After crumpling the wrappers and cardboard trays from their lunch, Frank and Joe threw them at the nearest garbage can. Frank's wad of trash came apart in midair, half of it falling behind the can, the other half bouncing off the front of it. Frank walked over to pick up the debris from his shot.

"I can see you're not planning a career in basketball," Joe said with a laugh.

Frank shook his head, then pulled a map of the zoo out of his back pocket. The San Diego Zoo was so large that visitors were given maps when they bought their tickets at the front gate.

Frank unfolded the map to its full size. "So, where to next?" he asked as he tried to find where they were.

Joe looked around at the different trails leading off from the snack area.

"We came here mainly to see the pandas, didn't we?" he said. "Why not head over there?"

"Good idea," Frank answered. After locating the panda house on the map, the brothers were on their way. Both brothers had traveled extensively, yet neither had ever seen a live panda.

"I can't wait to see these guys up close," Joe said.

"Not too close-up, though," Frank answered. "They may look like cuddly stuffed animals, but pandas have large, powerful teeth and claws."

The Hardys knew that the Republic of China, the only country in the world where pandas could be found outside of zoos, rarely lent any of its pandas out to other nations. As long as the San Diego Zoo had acquired a pair of pandas, Frank and Joe wanted to get a good look at the rare creatures while they had the chance.

Less than a minute after their search began, the two boys spotted a sign pointing the way to the panda exhibit.

"I think this means the dynamic Hardy brothers have succeeded once again," Joe announced.

Frank chuckled. "No challenge too great or too small, right, little brother?"

Joe was just about to comment on Frank calling him "little" when suddenly a loud crashing sound from the direction of the panda house caught their attention. Frank noticed that the crowd around them had all turned toward the noise, too.

"What was that?" Joe asked Frank.

"I don't know," Frank answered. "But maybe we should find out."

"Good idea," Joe said as he broke into a run, heading toward the panda house.

The two boys managed to move only a dozen steps, however, when they heard another loud smashing sound. This crash was accompanied by the sound of a car engine.

As the Hardys slowed down a bit, a truck came whipping around from behind the panda house, breaking through a chain strung across the driveway that said No Admittance.

The truck slammed against a bench as it made a wild turn, crumpling its rear fender and smashing the bench to pieces. Just then a zoo attendant came running out from behind the panda exhibit. Frank noticed that he was holding his hand up to his forehead, trying to stop a stream of blood.

"Stop, thieves! Somebody stop them!" the attendant called.

Frank and Joe charged toward the truck. Just then the truck made another reckless turn that put it on a collision course with the Hardys!

Chapter
Four

"Move, Joe!" Frank shouted. *"Move!"*

Joe Hardy scrambled as fast as he could, while Frank dove to the right of the wide zoo walkway. Both were desperate to get out of the path of the oncoming truck.

The vehicle roared on past the brothers and headed into the main area of the zoo. The driver blared the horn of the old truck but did not slow down despite the crowds of adults and children in his way. It was obvious to Joe that the driver was not ready to give anyone in his way any more time than he had the Hardy brothers to clear a path. Merely getting out of the truck's path was not all Joe Hardy had in mind.

Before the truck passed Joe completely, he was in motion, leaping for the back end of the racing vehicle. He hit the speeding truck at an awkward angle. The impact knocked the air from his lungs as he slammed up against the truck's flapping tailgate.

"Hang on, Joe!" Frank shouted as he struggled to his feet.

Joe could just barely hear his brother over the roar of the truck. He had just caught the edge of the tailgate with the fingers of one hand, his heel wedged between the bumper and the vehicle's tail wall. His body slammed back and forth for a moment, but then he managed to get his other arm securely over the back edge of the truck. He hung on desperately.

"Stay with it, Joe!" Frank shouted.

The truck was headed down the walkway in the direction from which he and his brother had just come. Joe watched as Frank took off and cut through the trees to follow them.

These guys are going to kill people if someone doesn't stop them, he thought. And right now, someone looks like *us*. Keep going, big brother. I have a hunch I know what you're up to.

Joe guessed Frank was hoping to cut the stolen truck off at the next turn. The zoo's paths were meant for strolling, not for drag racing. The walkways were wide enough to accommodate vehicles, of course, but not ones moving at extreme speeds—something Joe could tell the driver of the stolen truck was rapidly discovering from the way its speed was decreasing.

Despite the drop in acceleration, Joe could barely maintain a hold, hanging off the rear of the truck because of the driver's wild steering. In the truck bed, Joe could see the load of potted trees bouncing around wildly.

Several trees overturned and slapped down on Joe before hanging out over the tailgate. The driver had barely gotten the truck under control before he ran the left side of the vehicle over the shoulder of the road. The truck ground into the loose sand and scrub grass at the verge, its wheels catching for a moment. The vehicle jerked and slowed, skidding to the right, letting Joe know the driver was struggling to maintain control.

That's it, Joe thought, finally able to get a better grip as the truck slowed down. Just a few more seconds and I'm going to be on you guys like explosions in a summer blockbuster movie.

Joe struggled, his task now made harder by the trees lying on their sides, their top branches sticking out over the end of the truck. Joe smashed at them and pushed his way upward with all the strength he had. But before he could make it all the way over the tailgate to the relative safety of the truck bed, he saw the reflection of the vehicle's driver in the rear-view mirror. The driver appeared to be in his forties.

He was shouting at someone else in the front seat of the truck, but Joe could not hear what the man was saying. He watched the pair through the back window of the cab. At the same moment Joe's eyes met the driver's gaze. A wave of terror shot through Joe as something else caught his eye.

The passenger in the front seat unbuckled his seat belt and turned as he pulled a large handgun out from his jacket.

The man then leaned out the passenger side window as far as he could. He cocked the automatic and took aim at Joe just as Joe was beginning to pull himself into the truck bed through the overturned trees.

Joe stopped climbing in as the first two lead slugs blasted just past the side of his head. Hanging on by one hand, Joe tried desperately to shift his shaky handhold to the rear bumper of the truck. His fingers caught on the rusting metal, breaking away the looser pieces. His skin tore on the sharp edges left behind.

The truck hit a speed bump, and the trees in

the truck bed bounced up and crashed down, shaking the entire vehicle. The branches of several of them swatted Joe, almost knocking his shaky hold on the truck loose.

Wish I knew what they will try next, Joe thought. Guess there's only one way to find out. If there's anyone out there who likes me, this would be a great time to prove it.

His brief wish for luck made, Joe stuck his head around the side of the truck.

Bam! Bam!

Two more bullets whizzed past his head. He narrowly ducked in time to avoid the flying lead, but couldn't dodge the bullets and maintain his shaky hold on the rusting bumper at the same time.

"Oh, nuts!" he screamed, his cut and bleeding fingers losing their grip despite his best efforts.

When Joe fell, his left knee hit the ground first, his pants ripping and the skin of his knee scraping and tearing. Joe flipped on impact, his back striking the ground next. He gasped for air as his face and elbows, shoulders and hips slammed against the ground savagely. The shock knocked the wind from him.

Joe stayed where he had fallen, struggling to orient himself. At the same time he could see Frank dragging a pair of snack bar tables into the middle of the roadway just ahead of the truck.

The driver spun the steering wheel in an attempt to dodge the makeshift blockade. Unable to hold the turn, the truck slammed into the side of the snack bar and ground to a halt.

Frank ran forward and yanked open the door on the driver's side. The driver, still wearing his seat belt, had managed to escape injury.

His partner wasn't so lucky, Frank noticed. The other man wasn't wearing his seat belt. His head, it appeared to Frank, had bounced off the windshield with such force that he had crazed the glass into a spider's web of pellets.

Frank pulled the driver out from behind the wheel as Joe ran up to the truck. Both brothers spotted the gun in the driver's hand at the same time, and Frank threw a punch at the man.

The force of the blow caused him to drop his weapon, but the driver shook off the effects of Frank's punch quickly. Frank swung again, but the man blocked his punch and the next one as well.

At the same time, the passenger came to. From the cab of the truck, he raised his gun and took aim at Frank.

"Watch out!" Joe shouted. Joe was close enough to see the second man begin to tighten his finger on the trigger. Joe's warning startled the man, and he fired wildly, the bullet striking no one.

"Yahoo!" Joe shouted. "Score one for our team!"

The driver swung his leg around, knocking Frank's legs out from under him. As Frank fell, the driver retrieved his gun, sprang back into the stolen truck, and slammed it into reverse.

"Get up, Frank!" Joe shouted. "Get out of the way!"

Moving as quickly as he could, Frank crawled frantically to the side of the road, as the truck roared past him in reverse. The brothers were too battered to do anything further.

In truth, there was nothing they could do except watch the two thieves escape and be grateful they were alive themselves.

The zoo employee whom Frank and Joe had first seen chasing the truck caught up to them after a few moments. Out of breath, the older man panted as he tried to speak to the Hardy brothers.

"How's your head?" Joe asked, noting the groundsman's bloody forehead.

"Oh, that's okay," he said. "Looks worse than it is. It's really only a cut."

"Good," Frank added. "But we'd better get to a phone to call the police."

"Don't worry," the man told them. "I already called nine-one-one. Fat lot of good it'll do, of course. Those guys are long gone."

"I know," Frank muttered. "For all the good we did."

"You did a lot," the man answered. "Those guys could have injured lots of pedestrians. You stopped them."

"Thank us when we catch them," Joe said.

"Maybe we did do some good," Frank said. "But I don't get it. I mean, those guys shot at us—they tried to kill us and who knows how many other people, and for what?"

"Beats me," the zoo employee said. "As far as I know, all they stole was my truck."

"What was on the truck?" Joe asked. "Anything important—anything valuable?"

"Just the bamboo plants for the pandas," answered the man.

"That's it?" Frank asked. "Just plants?"

"Nothing more than a few tools, maybe. Couple of garden hoses. But that's it. It was just an old truck."

"What?" Joe asked in a stunned voice. "We almost died trying to stop a bamboo heist? I don't get it. Who risks their lives just to steal bamboo?"

"I don't know, Joe," Frank said. "You want to find out?"

Joe turned to his brother and smiled. "Yeah, I think I just might."

Chapter

Five

HEY, GUYS," Nancy asked, "how about dropping me off at the hotel? I'd like to do a few things."

"Sure," Anthony said. "Bess and I are going back to the convention for only a little while, anyway."

Nancy watched Anthony's car pull away. She thought that both he and Bess had seemed pleased to drop her off. She was happy, too, because it gave her a chance to do some investigating.

Once alone in her room, Nancy called the local police departments to determine who was responsible for the Dubchek murder.

It took Nancy only a few calls to find the

correct police precinct. Finding the detective in charge of the case, Nancy asked if she might have a moment of his time. The officer, a Detective Vickler, said he needed to interview some of the people from the conference and that if she came to his office right then, he would wait for her.

One twenty-minute cab ride later, Nancy was being shown into an interview room by an officer who said Nancy was expected. She sat at the table in the center of the room as the uniformed officer told her, "Detective Vickler will be with you in just a minute."

Nancy glanced at her watch, wondering how long she would really be kept waiting. Exactly fifty-eight seconds later, a large, powerfully built man walked in and introduced himself as Lieutenant T-Bone Vickler.

"Excuse me, detective," Nancy asked as they shook hands, "but before we begin, could I ask you a personal question?"

"You don't have to ask," the detective said. "Everybody who meets me wants to know the same thing—why do they call you T-Bone? Right?"

Nancy smiled and shrugged. The man smiled back and then told her, "It's all right. Like I said, everybody asks. It's no big deal . . . it's just that here in the land of tofu and bean sprouts, I seem to be the only man left in the world who still has the guts to eat beef."

Nancy chuckled. She appreciated the joke, and she could tell the detective liked people who appreciated his jokes. She could also tell that he had warmed to her.

The detective slid into a seat across the table from Nancy. He asked her a number of questions that would help him when he filled out the preliminary reports he needed to file before he could go further with his investigation.

They were all simple questions, mostly dealing with the kind of conference they were attending, why Carl Dubchek had been asked to attend it, what connection everyone involved had to the conference and to one another, and so forth. Nancy answered honestly, helping the detective as best she could.

Once they had finished, Vickler said, "All right—now I just want to recap your answers here. To the best of your knowledge, Carl Dubchek was a resident of Los Angeles. He was one of the United Nations' coordinators for their environmental conference being held here in this city. The conference is officially over, and most everyone will be leaving within the next few days. Correct?"

"Yes, sir," Nancy said.

"You don't know why he was asked to be a

coordinator, simply that he was an expert on Chinese studies. You don't know of any enemies he might have had. But you do know where he was headed this afternoon at the time of his death—a restaurant, for which you gave me the address."

"I'm afraid I don't know much more," Nancy said.

"No, no," Vickler answered. "Don't apologize. I have to thank you, Ms. Drew, for being so cooperative with the police. So, now that you've proved yourself to be a tourist and earned the gratitude of T-Bone Vickler, for whatever that's worth to a girl, tell me, what I can do for you."

Nancy quickly reviewed her relationships with both Bess and Anthony Green for the detective. She let him know just enough to think he understood why she was asking her questions. Nancy had met enough police officers to know that a rare few were ever very keen on having outsiders help them solve their cases.

Not having the time to worry about the egos of the entire Los Angeles police department, however, Nancy asked T-Bone if he or any other officers had been contacted by Anthony Green.

"Name doesn't ring any bells. I've already gone over the inquiry sheets—the lists we keep here at the station of people who call about crimes. Believe it or not, a lot of criminals will actually call the police to check on crimes they committed, trying to get information on how close we are to catching them."

"I've heard that before," Nancy answered. "And, not to suggest that she's a criminal, how about a Mrs. Grunderson? She's another of the conference coordinators."

"Yeah, I remember her," Vickler answered. "She's the one I spoke to when we called the conference. I just informed her of the deceased's condition. One of my men did speak with her at the convention center."

The lieutenant flipped through a report he had brought in with him. As he skimmed it for information, he told Nancy, "Says here she was very cooperative, but apparently she didn't even know as much about the deceased as you did."

"How about—" Nancy started to give Vickler another name, but the detective cut her off, telling her, "I can make this easy on you. So far, no one from the outside has called us on this case . . . except you, of course."

Strike one, Anthony, Nancy thought, her eyes narrowing slightly.

"Something wrong?" T-Bone asked.

"No, no," Nancy said, noting that the detective was a keenly perceptive man. "I'm just a little surprised that no one else was concerned enough to call. Could you tell me how Mr. Dubchek was killed?"

"Two forty-five-caliber bullets in the chest. We don't have a motive, but it's clearly a drive-by shooting. Nothing accidental about it, if that's what you were thinking."

"Was it a robbery?" Nancy asked.

"No," T-Bone said. "His watch, a ring, his wallet—cash and plastic still intact—even his briefcase was still with him when he was discovered. If anybody stole anything from him, I couldn't begin to guess what it was. But I don't think anything was taken."

"How could you tell?" Nancy asked.

"We can't be one hundred percent sure. But his pockets weren't turned inside out. His jacket was still buttoned. There were no smears in the blood found on the scene. There was nothing to indicate anyone had tampered with the body," T-Bone said.

Nancy decided to test the waters with a bold statement. "He was a lawyer for the United Nations. I wonder if this was an assassination?" She looked at T-Bone evenly to gauge his reaction.

"A surprising notion," the detective said. Suddenly the warmth fled T-Bone's eyes. Staring at Nancy with a cold look, "You're not some reporter, are you—TV, evening news? I don't need any—"

"I'm not a reporter, Detective Vickler," Nancy answered quickly. "Honest. Just a conference attendee who was supposed to have lunch with Carl Dubchek today."

She opened her small purse and held it out for the lieutenant to inspect. "No tape recorder. No notepad," she said. "In fact, although I did get to hear Mr. Dubchek speak at two different lectures, I never actually got to meet him face-to-face. He was murdered on his way to join my friends and me for lunch. I just wanted to . . . well, I'm sorry, you probably know what I mean."

Nancy could see from T-Bone's softened expression that he was no longer feeling threatened. Recognizing a good time to leave, Nancy stood and extended her hand to the detective, thanking him for being so helpful.

"That's supposed to be my line, but—okay, you're welcome," T-Bone said with a chuckle.

"Well," Nancy said, "I suppose I should be going. I'm certain you have plenty of important things to do."

The detective showed Nancy to the door, then opened it for her. Nancy nodded courteously, but just as she passed out into the hall, she paused and turned to the detective. "If I could just bother you with one more question," she said. "Does the name Cinder mean anything to you?"

"No—doesn't ring any bells," he said after a moment's thought. "Can you give me an idea what it might mean? And can I ask you why you're asking me?"

"It's nothing, really. Just something I heard earlier today."

"Un-huh." T-Bone moved into the hall and stood blocking Nancy's way. He eyed her with mild suspicion again. "You know, I wouldn't say that you were a bad person or anything, but . . . you wouldn't be keeping secrets from me, would you?"

"Detective Vickler," Nancy told him, "if I knew anything that you could use in your investigation, I would tell you immediately."

Vickler nodded and moved out of Nancy's way so she could leave. Then, after she had taken a few steps past him, he called out to her, stopping her.

"Hey, Ms. Drew, let me give you a little advice. While you're out there looking for something that could help my investigation, don't get yourself backed into a corner by anyone you can't handle. I'd hate to see one of the ugly things we have crawlin' around this town do you any harm."

"Me, too, detective," she answered honestly. "Me, too."

"So, Tony," Nancy asked before Anthony could enter Nancy and Bess's first-floor hotel room, "why is it the Los Angeles police have never heard of you?"

Anthony stopped dead in the doorway and stared at Nancy with surprise. "What are you talking about?" he asked and, moved into the room.

"They have no record of your calling them, and they never called you. They talked only to Mrs. Grunderson—and me."

"Nancy!" Bess shouted. "What's going on?"

"I've been doing a little investigating, Bess," Nancy answered, not taking her eyes off Anthony as she spoke. "There's a little bit too much wrong here, and I'm afraid we have to find out what it is."

Nancy stared at Anthony as she said, "Carl Dubchek was assassinated, wasn't he?"

"How? I mean . . ." Anthony sat down in the straight-back chair at the desk near the window. Eyes staring at the floor, he bent his head down. Nancy continued, hoping to get to the truth as quickly as possible.

"The police described Mr. Dubchek's murder as a drive-by killing. A car goes by and Carl Dubchek gets two bullets in the chest. But we all know what that might mean. Do you know why he was killed, Tony?"

"You know something about Mr. Dubchek's murder, Tony?" Bess asked.

"I didn't mean—"

"Stop it, Tony," Nancy said. "No excuses. This isn't some game. A U.N. lawyer and retired professor isn't your typical assassination target. Carl Dubchek was something more—wasn't he?"

Anthony shook his head back and forth. Nancy actually felt sorry for him as she watched his shoulders shake. Then he pulled himself together and quietly answered her question.

"He was a CIA agent."

Bess opened her mouth to speak, then closed it again.

Still staring at the floor, Anthony continued to talk. "It was a long time ago, when he was with the CIA. He's always been a lawyer, specializing in international law—specifically Far Eastern law. That's why the CIA recruited him—he was their main source for Asian facts, especially Chinese ones."

Before she could question him further, Bess suddenly moved forward and asked, "Why did you lie to me? *How* could you lie to me? Was everything you told me a lie?"

"Oh, no," Anthony protested. He stood up and put his hands on Bess's shoulders. Then he stared directly into her eyes. "At first, when the plan was in operation, I couldn't tell you everything. But everything I said about us—I meant all of that."

"What plan?" Nancy asked. "Who are you, really?"

Anthony didn't answer Nancy. Still staring into Bess's eyes, he said. "Everything changed when I met you. I've never known anyone like you, Bess. I couldn't go through with it. I had to protect you."

"Protect me?" Bess asked. "From what?"

"From Cinder," Anthony said.

Hearing the mysterious name again, Nancy asked, "Who is Cinder, Tony?"

Shame filling his face, Anthony turned to Nancy. Just as he opened his mouth to begin speaking, a loud motor and screeching tires sounded out in the parking lot.

"What's going on?" Nancy asked, crossing the room to join Anthony and her friend near the window.

Earlier, when Anthony and Bess dropped her off, it had started raining again. Nancy had closed the curtains, not wanting to look out over the dark, rain-swept parking lot. What she saw now when she opened the curtains was far worse than a few rain clouds.

"Bess! Tony!" she screamed as she saw a sleek red sports car speed toward them. "Get down!"

Nancy threw herself backward, angling her fall so that she would land behind the room's huge easy chair. A score of shots roared through the room. Glass and metal splattered everything. Plaster exploded in all directions, gouged out of the walls in huge chunks by the spray of bullets.

Nancy pressed herself into the rug and didn't know exactly when the car roared off. After only a moment she did sense that the shooting had ceased and that the car must have left.

"Bess," Nancy cried as she scrambled to her feet. "Bess—are you okay?"

Nancy started to cross the room but stopped at the sight of blood on the carpet. She gasped at what she saw next. Lying motionless on the carpet were Bess and Anthony Green!

Chapter

Six

"WELL," FRANK SAID, smiling for the first time in hours, "here's something interesting."

Getting up from the laptop he and Joe had brought with them, he stretched his arms. On the other side of the room, Joe sat up on his bed, half asleep.

Joe covered a massive yawn. "It better be truly interesting if it's going to keep me awake," he said.

"Oh, I think this will keep you awake," Frank answered.

After their run-in with the bamboo thieves, they had spent several hours with the San Diego police going over mug shots in the hope of identifying the two thugs. Unfortunately, neither they nor the zoo employee spotted anyone they recognized.

By the time the brothers left the police station, it was growing dark. The police they had just left were all going off duty, content to leave the mystery of the bamboo thieves for the next day. The Hardys, though, had other plans.

Frank and Joe had both been happy to find that Internet access was provided to hotel guests. Now, after several hours hunched over the keyboard, Frank was exhausted but pleased at what he had found.

"So?" Joe asked, yawning as he crossed the room. "What have you got?"

Pointing toward the screen, Frank said, "Look at this."

Joe sat down at the desk, staring at the screen. He scrolled up and down the questions and answers Frank had sent and received over the last hour, but nothing out of the ordinary jumped out at him.

"Frank, whatever it is you're waiting for me to get, I'm not seeing it."

"Sorry, Joe," Frank answered. "You're still half asleep. Let me walk you through it. Go up to my first question."

As Joe scrolled back to the first screen, he asked, "Who did you find to answer questions about bamboo at this time of night?"

"Believe it or not, I got a student worker at the Department of Natural Studies in Hong Kong. He filled me in on everything we were wondering about."

"Okay, great," Joe responded. "So start walking me through this."

"Right," Frank answered. "Well, first off, I managed to identify the guns the thieves were using. One was pointed right at me—I did get a pretty good look at it."

"And your student in Hong Kong told you what you saw?" Joe asked.

"Sorry—guess I'm tired, too. No, I got that earlier. I found a Web page dedicated to foreign gun manufacturers that came complete with pictures. It turns out our playmates' weapons were produced by Norinco—"

"The old Chinese Communist state-owned weapons makers," Joe said.

"Right, it was their knock-off of the Russian Makarov. They just call it the Type fifty-nine." Frank took a swallow from a glass of water on the desk. Setting it back down, he continued.

"The thing is, it's not that common a gun for someone to come across here in the United States. But it *is* a standard issue sidearm for Chinese military officers."

Suddenly Joe was wide awake. "This puts a whole new light on things. Go on."

"Because," Frank said, just as excited as his brother, "you're wondering what Chinese soldiers or secret agents would be doing at the San Diego Zoo stealing bamboo out of their own pandas' mouths, right?"

"You got it," Joe said. "So, what's the answer?"

"I'm not sure," Frank had to admit. "But I have an idea. Li—he's the student in Hong Kong—told me there's nothing valuable about bamboo itself. It's actually a member of the grass family. Some varieties can grow over a foot in a single day, and it can grow almost anywhere."

"But we quizzed the zoo guy about the pots of bamboo those guys stole," Joe said. "He was sure there wasn't anything valuable hidden in them."

Joe scratched his head. "The pots were old. They'd been around the zoo for years. It had to be the bamboo those thieves were after."

"Correct, professor," Frank said. "When I laid the whole story out to Li, he suggested that maybe these guys had a panda of their own to feed."

"What?" Joe looked at his brother. "Where would they get a panda? I thought the Chinese government kept tight control over all the pandas in the world."

"They do," Frank answered as he pulled up the extra chair and sat down to face his brother. Frank took another gulp of water.

"Li said that it takes pandas a long time to learn to eat anything except bamboo. The ones in zoos do eventually eat all sorts of things—fish, apples, milk, and eggs. He even told me about a couple that like baked potatoes and spaghetti. But that's beside the point. What's important is that there's only one thing that can make bamboo valuable, and that's if you've got a panda to feed that isn't used to captivity."

"Interesting," Joe said. He took a bottle of fruit juice out of the tiny refrigerator in their room while his mind raced. "So, the next thing you did was check around for stories about panda abductions, right?"

"You got it," Frank answered. "That's when I woke you up."

"Somebody stole a panda somewhere?" Joe asked.

"No. Not yet, at least. Right now there are only twenty-seven zoos in the world that have pandas in captivity. And most of those are inside China. None of them have reported any thefts. And everyone from Interpol to our contacts in the Network says that they haven't heard anything about anyone trying to smuggle a panda out of China."

"Then what's going on?" Joe asked.

"While I was digging around on the Web, we got some E-mail."

"So?" Joe's face was blank. "We get E-mail all the time."

"That's true," Frank said. "But we don't usually get instant messages from people who know we're doing a Web search."

Joe snapped his fingers. "Someone saw your inquiries and got curious," he said.

"Go to the head of the class," Frank answered as he reached over for the mouse. He clicked on several different icons until he had reopened the mailbox entry he had read just before waking his brother. "Take a look."

Joe read the message that had been sent to their E-mail address. The sender was indeed curious about who was looking for reports of bamboo and panda-related crimes and what the interest was.

Joe read the E-mail identification slug line. It only took him a second to remember what it meant. Often in cases that dealt with crimes such as espionage or international terrorism, Joe and his brother had come in contact with an individual known as the Gray Man. An official of the hypersecret, high-tech government agency known as the Network, the Gray Man had passed on valuable information to the Hardys, including a list of E-mail screen names that identified the senders as members of other government agencies.

"This came from the CIA," Joe said excitedly. Eagerly he began to tap away at the keyboard, sending their questioner a reply. As he did, he told his brother, "Well, they've been so kind to come a-calling—let's see what they want."

Joe quickly fashioned a response several paragraphs long. He identified himself and Frank, then related the story of what had happened to the two of them earlier at the zoo. He added that he and Frank were looking into the crime and that anything the CIA could do to help them would be greatly appreciated.

Frank read the message over Joe's shoulder while his brother was inputting it. As soon as it was finished, Frank said, "Looks good to me. Send it, and let's see what they have to say."

Joe clicked on the Send icon. "Well," he said, "there's no telling how long it's going to take them to get back to us. I'm going to brush my teeth and take a shower while I have the chance."

Joe was still brushing when the automatic mail alert sounded, letting them know they had an answer.

"That was fast," Frank said. Sliding into the chair in front of the computer, he grabbed the mouse to open the mail.

"Yeah, a little bit *too* fast if you ask me," Joe called out from the bathroom. He spit a mouthful of toothpaste foam into the sink. "So, come on, spill it—what did they say?"

"Not much," Frank answered. "They're claiming it's a matter of national security."

"National security?" Joe answered from the bathroom. "Stealing bamboo comes under the heading of national security? Are they kidding or what?"

"You got me," Frank said. "They just say that they were watching the Web for questions about pandas and bamboo, and that they're following up on anyone who fits a certain profile."

Joe stalked out of the bathroom and came up behind Frank. He read the monitor screen over his brother's shoulder.

"Send them another message," Joe said. "Tell them we'd like to talk to the agent in charge of this bamboo and panda watch of theirs."

"Good idea," Frank said. He started typing again. He sent the request and was rewarded with an almost instantaneous response.

"What'd they say?" asked Joe.

"They say we can't talk to the agent in charge of the project," Frank replied.

"Oh, yeah, there's a surprise," Joe said with annoyance. "Did they say why?"

"Actually," Frank answered, "they did. They say we can't talk to him because he was just murdered."

Chapter
Seven

THERE'S NOT MUCH more you can do here,"
Lieutenant Vickler told Nancy. "Why don't you
go back and get some rest?"

Nancy stared down at Bess, unable to answer
the lieutenant. Her friend had been unconscious since the accident at the hotel. When the
first squad cars had arrived at the scene, Nancy
asked for Vickler. She was relieved to see the
lieutenant waiting when she arrived at the hospital with the ambulances.

"At least your friend lived," Vickler said. "In
fact, she didn't even get shot. Just hit her head
on the edge of the desk and got a concussion.
The doctors said she should be fine in a day or

so. That's a whole lot better than what happened to Green."

Nancy shuddered. Anthony had been killed by the hail of bullets that had torn apart the hotel room. His body had protected Bess from taking any bullets.

I just have to wait here, Nancy thought.

As if reading her mind, Vickler said, "It's going to be all right."

When the lieutenant had questioned Nancy about the shooting, she felt foolish not having more information about what happened. She hadn't been able to get a clear view of the driver of the car or any of its passengers. Nor had she been able to get a look at the license plate.

"I'm sorry," she said, "but when I saw the car coming at us—saw the guns sticking out the windows—I just ducked."

Nancy stared down at Bess once more, taking in the intravenous drip connected to her arm. "I just ducked and left my best friend to get shot."

"Now, you listen here, Ms. Drew," Vickler said. "You've got to stop beating yourself up over this. You got the color of the car, the make, and the model. Most people wouldn't remember anything but the guns."

"That doesn't help Bess, though," Nancy answered. "Does it?"

"And just what were you supposed to do for

her?" Raising his voice a notch, the lieutenant asked, "Tell me—what could you have done? If you had tried to do anything, you might have been the one torn apart by the bullets. We took seven bullets out of the walls of the room. That's a lot of lead flying around."

"I still don't understand why you won't let me help you look into this," Nancy told the lieutenant.

"Because," he answered, "I don't know what 'this' is. Who were those guys trying to kill? You? It *was* your room. But the hotel manager said that Green had left word at the front desk that he'd be in your room. There was also an outside call that came in trying to locate him. Seems like someone was verifying he was where he said he'd be so they could come after him."

Holding up the fingers of one hand, the detective used them to count off the possibilities. "One," he said, "could be they just wanted you. Two, could be they wanted Mr. Green. Three, maybe they wanted you and Bess. Four, maybe they waited for Mr. Green and Bess to come in because they wanted all three of you."

"But how would they know that?" Nancy asked. "And why would anyone want to hurt any of us?"

"Why did anyone want to hurt Carl Dubchek?" When Nancy didn't answer, Vickler said, "No, it's best if you stay out of this."

"I don't know why you feel that way," Nancy protested. "I mean, it's not like I don't know my way around an investigation."

"Listen," Vickler answered, "if I hadn't gotten the glowing report on you from the River Heights Police Department, you'd be a suspect in this investigation."

"You checked up on me?" Nancy asked.

"It's my job. Remember?"

Nancy nodded. "But your job is also to find out what's going on around here. Who was Anthony Green—really? What was he up to? Was he using Mr. Dubchek, or even the United Nations, for something?"

"I don't know the answers yet," Vickler said. "But it's my job to find out. And it's also my job not to endanger any citizens. You're upset because you've just seen your best friend get hurt. You're feeling responsible and helpless and guilty."

"That's not fair, T-Bone—" Nancy began.

"No," the detective said before Nancy could continue, "it's not at all fair. I lost a partner once. He was killed in a shootout at a liquor store. Four of them, twenty-five of us. You'd think the crooks would've been smart enough to figure the odds on that one, but they weren't."

Vickler turned away from Nancy for a moment. Nancy could tell he was remembering that night. "For a twenty-dollar robbery they thought they should shoot it out. We had to kill two of them. One surrendered. One got away."

The lieutenant turned and looked at Nancy. "Do you think I was feeling any less bad then than you are now? Do you think my superiors let me go out looking for that last punk? No, they didn't. And they were right not to. You're too torn up right now. You let us take care of this. Sit this one out. It's for the best."

Vickler turned and headed out of the room. Nancy watched him leave, watched the door swing shut behind him. Then, when she was certain he was gone, she looked down at Bess once more and whispered, "Don't you worry, Bess—I'll find out what this is all about. And I'll get the people who did this to you and Tony. With or without the police knowing about it."

Reaching down, Nancy pulled the blanket that was half-covering Bess a bit higher. Then, she headed for the door. With her hand on the knob, she turned back to her friend for one last moment.

"I'll get them," she said with conviction. "You can count on it."

Back at her hotel, Nancy checked into the new room the manager had given her, then headed for the crime scene that had been her room that morning. She hadn't returned her key, claiming it had been lost in the excitement. Now she used it to reenter her old room, carefully maneuvering her way past the bright yellow crime scene tape that had been stretched across the doorway.

Easing the door closed behind her, Nancy turned on the lights. Then she stood off to one side and scrutinized everything in the room, one object at a time.

She didn't exactly know what she was looking for, but like any good investigator, she knew she had to get an overview before she began. The scene of the crime seemed the most logical place to begin, she decided.

Detectives had removed all of the personal items that belonged to her and Bess and had taken them to their new room. Now the room where Bess had been hurt and Green had been killed was just an impersonal hotel cube.

And, Nancy told herself, somewhere in it is something that's going to point me in the right direction.

Nancy scanned the room, her eyes passing over every piece of broken glass and splintered furniture. As she did, Nancy pieced together everything she knew, looking to see what it all might mean.

"Fact," she said aloud. "Carl Dubchek was

murdered in the street by men who shot him and drove away. Just the way they shot at us. Fact, Dubchek was an ex-CIA agent. Fact, Anthony was up to something that concerned Carl Dubchek, something he was afraid was going to involve Bess. He had started to tell us what it was when we were attacked and he was killed. He said it had to do with that person I heard him talking to on the phone—Cinder."

Nancy assumed that Cinder was a code name, which fit in with Dubchek's having been a CIA agent. She knew that whatever was going on had to be connected to Carl Dubchek—it had to. Maybe, she thought, Dubchek had been working with the agency again.

"So, now all I have to do is prove it. Great," she muttered. Her eyes swept the room. "And just how do I do that?"

Then her gaze came to rest on the couch. Somehow her unconscious mind had noticed something her conscious mind had not yet realized.

As Nancy stared at the couch, she quietly asked herself, "What is it? What is it that's wrong?"

The only thing different about the couch from when she'd checked in a few days earlier was the bullet through the center cushion. But there were bullet holes everywhere. Nancy looked at each of them—two over the couch, one beside the lamp, three beside the couch, a last one between the couch and the door.

"Seven," she said aloud. Just as Vickler told me, she thought to herself. Surprising that they could shoot off so many rounds and only these seven and the ones in Tony managed to come in through the window.

And then it hit her.

Vickler said the police removed seven bullets from the room, she thought. But if there's a hole in the couch . . .

Nancy grabbed the couch and moved it away from the wall. When she did, she was greeted by the sight of another hole in the wall. Staring at it for a moment, she whispered,

"Eight."

Smiling, Nancy took her room key from her pocket and used it to tear away at the plaster-board wall.

"So, what else could I show you?"

Nancy looked at the young forensics officer and smiled.

"Well," she told him, "there is one thing I'm curious about."

"Ask away," he told her. "We're here to help."

Nancy almost blushed. She didn't like having to trick law officers, but one of her two best friends was in the hospital and the police had refused to allow her to help with the investigation. She was going to find out what was going on no matter what she had to do.

"Are you sure you wouldn't mind answering my questions?" Nancy asked. "When my professor assigned me to do a paper on criminal investigation techniques, I never thought it could be so fascinating. But it's so late at night, and I'm taking up way too much of your time—"

"No, no, you're not," the young man protested. Nancy watched as he pushed at his tangled hair.

Nancy flashed her brightest smile. "Well, the one thing my professor said I should include in my paper is a section on comparison microscopes. Do you have one here?"

"Sure," the young man answered, obviously happy for any reason that kept Nancy in his office longer. "Right over here."

Without hesitation, he led her to a separate room. On a table built into the wall rested an oversize microscope, one with two sets of magnifying lenses.

Sitting before the bulky piece of equipment, the officer told Nancy, "This is it. It's a simple machine, really. You just take the things you want to compare and slide them under the two lenses. Then, you turn these knobs until you bring both objects into focus. The microscope lines the two up against each other in the viewer. If the two things are similar, you'll know it in just a few seconds."

"What kind of things can you compare with it?" Nancy asked. She already knew what the piece of equipment was used for and felt ridiculous pretending she didn't.

The young forensics man leaned forward, eager to answer Nancy's question. "There was an interesting case we had just a while back. We had a piece of wire fragment from a bomb. There were identifiable striations, that is, fracture markings, on it. We told the detectives in charge of the case that if they found any suspects, they should check the suspect's tools for a set of wire cutters. We were able to get a conviction by proving the guy made the bomb simply from the fact that his tool made the same kind of fractures as the ones found on the bomb fragment."

"That's fascinating," Nancy said. She noted the name plate pinned to his lapel as she asked, "So, would that be the main use for a comparison microscope, Officer Maren?"

"Oh, no," the officer said. "That was an exotic case. And, please, call me Wally."

"Okay," Nancy answered. "Wally."

The young forensics man blushed slightly. "Mostly, we do bullet match-ups," he said. "When a bullet is recovered from a crime scene, we save it until a weapon is found. Then a bullet fired from the weapon we suspect to be the one used in the crime is compared with the bullet from the crime scene. If they match, you know you have the gun that was used in the crime."

"Could I see how it works, Wally?" Nancy asked, holding her breath.

Happy for a chance to show off, the young man agreed to demonstrate the microscope instantly.

When he asked what she'd like to see, she told him, "Well, there was a story in the evening paper about a man being shot a couple of times in a drive-by shooting. If you recovered two bullets from his body, that would give us two bullets from the same gun, wouldn't it?"

"You mean the Dubchek shooting, don't you?"

"That was it," Nancy said, trying to sound casual.

The technician smiled and told Nancy that the case she mentioned just happened to be one being investigated by his precinct.

Nancy did not tell the young man that she already knew that. She simply smiled at her good fortune and sat back to wait while he went to get the bullets in question.

When the young man returned, Nancy asked, "Would it be okay if I held one, Wally? I've never actually held a bullet before."

The forensics man handed Nancy one of the two bullets that had slain Carl Dubchek. She pretended to be fascinated. Then, as the officer sat down at the comparison microscope, Nancy quickly switched the bullet he had given her for the one she had dug out of her hotel room wall.

Handing it to him, she watched while he slid it under the second set of lenses. Then, after a moment of adjusting the focus on the microscope, he invited Nancy to sit and have a look. She did.

Sitting down, she leaned over the microscope, looking through the eyepieces. What she saw were two burned, gray cylinders positioned side by side. Each was etched with multiple lines gouged into their sides—rifling from the inside of the gun barrel, Officer Maren explained.

Nancy, of course, didn't need the explanation. She knew what she was looking at right then.

What she was seeing was proof—proof that the same people who had murdered Carl Dubchek had blown apart her hotel room. Proof that whoever had killed the retired CIA agent had also killed Anthony Green and put Bess in the hospital.

"So," the forensics officer asked, "can you tell what you're looking at?"

"Oh, yes," Nancy answered aloud. "I can."

I can tell exactly what I'm looking at, she thought. I'm looking at trouble. I'm looking at proof that this is a lot bigger than the police think, and unless I miss my guess, there's going to be a whole lot more shooting—with me and Bess in the line of fire.

Chapter
Eight

MAN, DAD," FRANK SAID respectfully, "you make it look so easy."

"Glad to see the old man still has a few tricks he can pass on to his brilliant offspring," Fenton Hardy answered.

After the CIA had stonewalled Frank and Joe, giving them no additional information, they had gone down the hall to their father to ask his advice.

After Frank and Joe had presented their problem, Mr. Hardy accompanied them back to their room. He reviewed the messages they had traded with the CIA, quickly recognizing the government E-mail tag as belonging to the Central Intelligence Far East branch. He then instituted another search, this time of recent obituaries.

In less than an hour the trio of investigators had found a death notice for a lawyer and retired professor of international law, specializing in Chinese law.

"Interesting," Mr. Hardy said, "This Dubchek character looks like your best bet, guys. An assassination that has the police baffled. Someone with ties to the U.N."

"And he was killed just up the road, in Los Angeles," Joe added. "That's convenient."

"It's well over a hundred miles up to central Los Angeles, boys," their father corrected. "Not quite 'up the road,' I'd say."

"Close enough, though," Frank countered. "I mean, it's closer than if he got murdered in China."

"You've got me there," their father admitted. Mr. Hardy yawned loudly. "So, you guys going to poke around in this for a little while?"

"We were thinking about it," Frank answered. "If you don't need us here for anything."

"I brought you along to have a good time. If I know my boys, you probably couldn't have a better time than getting involved in an investigation."

"One that the CIA is mixed up in," Joe added. "Let's not forget them. Or those two punks who gave us the trouble at the zoo today."

"If they're connected to Dubchek, that is," Frank said. "Even though I have a hunch they are connected, it's best to proceed as if they're not, just so we don't miss anything by making bad assumptions."

"Hmm," Mr. Hardy said, rubbing the back of his neck, "maybe I don't have so much more left to teach you two after all."

"Well," Frank said, "I wouldn't mind getting your opinion on one thing."

"Shoot," their father answered.

"I've been thinking about those two thieves. Why do you think they'd make such a mess out of that robbery? I mean, they seemed pretty professional. At least as far as taking care of themselves goes. So, why pull an obvious broad daylight robbery that seemed to be from a Three Stooges movie?"

"Maybe it was just easier that way," Mr. Hardy suggested. "Nighttime security is tighter. Gates are locked. Perhaps these crooks had been hanging around and saw an opportunity and took it. The criminal mind can be hard to fathom sometimes. Especially when you don't know what the motives are."

Joe nodded his head in agreement as his father continued to talk.

"For all we know, they might not have

wanted bamboo at all," Mr. Hardy continued. "They simply could have needed a truck for some reason. You have to remember, as good as a theory is, until it's proven, it's just a theory."

"That's for sure," Joe said. He stretched out on his bed. "Give me a straightforward bank robber any day."

"You do think we're on the right track," Frank asked, "don't you, Dad?"

"I think so," Mr. Hardy said. "But you'll know better than I do soon enough."

Stretching his arms out, he rose from his chair and headed for the door. "Maybe that's why I'm leaving this one up to you two," he said, his hand on the doorknob. "That and the fact that I'm giving the closing speech at the convention luncheon tomorrow."

Mr. Hardy glanced at his watch. "I guess I mean later on today. So, I assume I won't be seeing your smiling faces at breakfast in a few hours?"

"You can count on that, Dad," Joe said. He got under the covers.

"You two be careful," Mr. Hardy said. He broke into a grin. "You know what your mother would say if I came home without you."

"Thanks, Dad," Frank and Joe answered in unison.

After their father was gone, Frank told his brother, "I think Dad's got a point."

"What do you mean?"

"The more I think about those two guys we tangled with today, the more I think there was something wrong about that whole setup. I've been getting the feeling that there was more going on there than a bamboo robbery."

"Like maybe they wanted people to know that someone was stealing bamboo," Joe asked. "Even if certain other parties—whose initials would be C, I, and A—might want to cover the fact up."

"That's exactly what I was thinking," Frank admitted.

"It's a good thought," Joe said, and sat up in bed, turning to his brother. "Do you think we might be out of our league on this one?" He hid a smile as he added, "I mean, murder in the streets, CIA cover-ups, international thieves . . . maybe this is too much for you, Frank, a high school senior who has to think about the future and all."

Frank tossed a pillow at his brother and turned out the lights. "Keep up the wisecracks and you won't have any future to think about."

"Well," Frank said, "this is going smoothly."

Joe didn't answer immediately because he was too caught up thinking about the rejection he and Frank had received from Lieutenant Vickler.

The brothers got into the car they had rented in San Diego. "Normally I'd wonder about a police officer who told us to stay away," Joe said. "I mean, the only law officers who ever gave us trouble over our looking into something were usually somehow involved with whatever crime was going on."

"I had the same feeling for a moment," Frank said.

"You think T-Bone might be one of the bad guys?" Joe asked.

"No, I'd bet he's a straight arrow. But I'd also bet there was something he wasn't telling us." Frank fastened his seat belt before turning the key in the ignition. "I'd sure like to know what it was."

"He's a Californian," Joe answered. "Maybe having to sleep through another night of rain made him grumpy today."

"Could be," Frank said. He laughed at the same time.

"Oh, hey, like it matters," Joe answered cheerfully. "We'll just solve this case without his help. Then he can explain to his captain why he wasn't smart enough to use us in the first place."

Frank pulled away from the curb. "You have the address where Carl Dubchek was murdered?" he asked.

"Sure." Joe sat forward and pulled his wallet

from his back pocket. Then he pulled the card he had written the address down on out of it. After that he opened the glove compartment and pulled out the Los Angeles map he had purchased when he and Frank had stopped for gas just outside the city.

Joe unfolded the map. "I take it we're going to take a little look at the crime scene?" he asked.

"As long as it's okay with Lieutenant Vickler," Frank answered.

Joe laughed and studied the map for a moment. "I'll ask permission the very next time I see him."

"You do that," Frank said, laughing as well. "But first, how about some directions?"

Joe had the best route to their destination figured out before Frank could reach the next traffic light.

Frank and Joe got out of their car. There were no other cars on the block. It was deserted.

"Did you ever see so much legal parking in your life?" Frank asked.

"Man," Joe commented, his eyes scanning left and right for some sign of recent police activity, "this place is a ghost town."

"There might be ghosts," Frank answered, "but where's the town?"

Joe nodded in silent agreement. Both he and

his brother had suspected they might find themselves in a deserted part of town when they got to the scene of Carl Dubchek's murder. As they had traveled from the precinct house, the neighborhoods around them had become less and less populated. Block by block, the carefully groomed palm trees and stylish buildings of downtown Los Angeles had become nonexistent.

By the time they reached the corner where the murder had taken place, there were nothing but vacant lots and boarded-up buildings.

Not willing to give up, Frank approached an elderly man sitting on the remains of what appeared to be a long-abandoned bus bench. "Excuse me, sir, could I talk to you for a few minutes?"

The man had trouble focusing his eyes, and after a long moment said, "What do you want?"

"A man was murdered here recently. I need to find the spot where it happened. I was wondering if you could direct me to it."

The man thought for a moment, then he answered simply, "For a dollar."

Frank considered the man's answer, then told him, "If you take us there, I'll give you two dollars."

The man thought for another few seconds, then stood up shakily. His only answer was "Okay." He started off down the cracked and broken sidewalk. He pointed to an abandoned lot littered with trash. "That's it," he said.

"Oh, yeah—sure," Joe said. "What? You think we were born yesterday?"

"No," Frank interrupted, reaching for his wallet. "Look over there."

Joe turned his head in the direction of his brother's hand. Instantly he spotted what Frank had—a cleared area in the center of the weeds that appeared to have been trampled down recently. Strips of yellow crime scene tape were clearly in evidence.

"Thanks, mister," Joe said. With the two dollars clutched tightly in his hand, the old man walked silently away, leaving the brothers to their investigation.

"Well," Frank said, "some things are becoming a bit clearer."

"You mean that the article we found about this shooting didn't have its facts straight?"

"Yeah. It's a lot easier to see why witnesses were so hard to find. This isn't exactly a heavily populated section of town."

Joe nodded. Unlike most of the city they had already seen, in this section the traffic was very light. Only a few cars moved up and down the street.

"Something else occurs to me," Joe said as he and Frank walked across the lot. "It's one thing when someone is gunned down in the middle of a busy street. Maybe that's a random shooting, maybe it isn't. But this?"

"And it makes me wonder," Frank said, "what was Dubchek doing in this neighborhood in the first place?"

"You're reading my mind," Joe said.

Frank noticed something silver colored sticking out of the ground. He held it up to inspect. "Now, what do we have here?"

"It's a gas cartridge," Joe said, turning the small metal cylinder over in his hand. "But what's it doing here?"

"There's enough trash in this lot so that it could be unrelated to the case," Frank said, "but I don't think so."

"No," Joe said. "Not within the crime scene."

Joe pointed out several things he had noticed. "Obviously no one draws a chalk outline in dirt, but look at how the weeds have been either crushed or cleared in this area, as well as the sets of footprints in the dried mud. It's clear a body was there. And look at how new all the heels look. Those aren't the shoes of the people who live in this neighborhood."

"Right," Frank answered. "I'm with you, but they could also be from the detectives who investigated the case."

Getting down on his knees beside his brother,

Frank studied the area where Carl Dubchek's body had recently lain. He was just about to make a point when he was stopped by the screeching of a car's tires somewhere in the distance. A female voice shouted at the same time but stopped abruptly as the racing engine sounds faded.

Frank looked at his brother and commented, "Nice neighborhood, huh?"

"Yeah, great," Joe said. "But let's get back to business. Look, see how the ground up here where we are is dried out from the rain already, but just a few feet down from us it's still moist. The ground slopes down from here."

Joe held up the cartridge and studied it once more. "The way it rained here in Los Angeles yesterday, this thing could have been uncovered and then slid downhill."

"It could have," Frank said. "Dubchek could have been holding it and dropped it. It was raining when he was killed yesterday afternoon."

"That's right," Joe added. "The weight of his body could have forced it into the mud. Then after a full night of rain it got uncovered."

"I think you could be right," Frank said.

"I think he's right, too," another voice echoed from the sidewalk. Still on their knees, the brothers turned their heads. What they saw was a man whose expensive suit and highly polished shoes marked him as an outsider to the neighborhood.

What they also saw was the heavy revolver in his hand and the silencer on the end of it. Sticking out his free hand, the man pointed toward the gas cartridge in Joe's hand.

"I'll take that," he said.

Then, raising his gun hand, he cocked the weapon and aimed it straight at Joe!

Chapter
Nine

So, what do you think of our little setup?" the young forensics officer asked.

"It's very interesting," Nancy answered. She looked out the wire-reinforced window of the forensics unit and shuddered as she reviewed the facts of the case so far. Carl Dubchek was an ex–CIA operative. He gets gunned down first, then whoever did it comes after Anthony Green. But does that mean this has something to do with the conference since they were both involved with it, or does something more sinister connect Dubchek and Anthony?

"I love it myself," the forensics man said, unaware that Nancy's thoughts were far away.

Nancy returned her attention to the young man.

"So, Wally, would there be more evidence connected to the same case on file here, or would the bullets be all you'd handle?" she asked.

"Oh, no—we have all the evidence here in the lab." Officer Maren walked back to where he had gotten the bullets. In a moment he returned with a thick file.

"This is everything we know at present about the case. Notes from the detectives on the scene, photos of the crime scene, fingerprint reports from the cartridges recovered. We have nothing conclusive yet, I'm afraid."

"Would you mind if I looked through this for a moment?" Nancy asked. "I mean, would it be all right?"

"I guess it would be okay," Maren said. "Take your time with it. I have to restock the dusting brushes in one of the mobile units. I'll be back in a second."

Nancy began to scan the pages as the young officer left the lab. The file was not of any great help to her outside of pinpointing the location of the crime scene.

It was clear to Nancy that the police had little to go on. The crime scene photos told her nothing that she didn't already know. She had seen Carl Dubchek, so the photographs did confirm that the man who had been killed was indeed the man she had heard lecture at the conference.

The police don't even seem to know that Mr. Dubchek was with the CIA, Nancy noted. At least they know where he was murdered. That gives me my first destination for tomorrow, she thought.

When Maren came back into the lab, Nancy returned the file to him.

"I can't thank you enough for all your help, Wally," she told him. "I've learned so much from you."

"That's all right," Maren told her. "Do you think that we could see each other again? Not so professionally, I mean?"

"Well, I'll probably be back here before you know it," Nancy answered. "Why don't we wait and see what happens?"

Nancy could tell from his sad expression that Officer Maren would rather have gotten a firm commitment for a date. She left the crime lab hoping she hadn't hurt the young man's feelings.

At that moment all she wanted to do was leave the station and go back to the hospital to check on Bess. Not only had she gotten all the information she wanted, but she also had no desire to run into Lieutenant Vickler. She understood his reasons for not wanting to help her—even sympathized with them. But she didn't want to listen to any more of his lectures or advice on staying out of harm's way.

What I want to do, she thought as she left the precinct house, is find out who put one of my best friends in the hospital and put them where they can't hurt anyone else.

Nancy made it to the hospital halfway through evening visiting hours. She sat with Bess for the rest of the time remaining, but there was no change in her friend's condition. After that, exhausted from her day, Nancy went back to her hotel.

First, she stopped for a quick dinner in the restaurant next to the hotel. She concentrated on what little she had learned to see if she could figure out anything she might have missed earlier. When she returned to the hotel she checked her messages. There was one from her father.

Nancy went up to her room quickly and called home. Her father picked up on the second ring.

"I'm impressed, Dad," she said with a laugh. "You beat Hannah to the phone."

Hannah Gruen had been with the Drew family ever since Nancy's mother had died, when Nancy was only three. "I knew you'd call when you got my message, so I arranged for her to be out tonight."

Nancy smiled. She knew she had the perfect father. Carson Drew was a noted criminal lawyer with a lightning-quick mind. Nancy knew she could always count on him to think of everything.

"Mr. Marvin called me after the hospital notified him of Bess's condition. How is she?"

Nancy gave her father a quick synopsis of everything that had happened. She made sure he knew that she was all right as well. Mr. Drew trusted his daughter completely and had faith in her sleuthing abilities. But Nancy also knew that even though he hadn't asked he would be concerned until she let him know she was all right.

"That's about all I can do tonight, Dad. Now I'm just going to take a fast shower and turn in early. I want to get a good night's sleep."

"All right, sweetheart," Mr. Drew said. "You just be careful."

"Now you're starting to sound like Lieutenant Vickler." Nancy laughed.

"I'm your father," Mr. Drew reminded Nancy. "I'm supposed to sound like this."

"I guess you are, Dad," Nancy responded. "But don't worry about me. Tell the people who put Bess in the hospital to be careful. They're the ones who *really* need that warning."

* * *

In the morning Nancy awoke feeling fresh and eager to get down to business. She ate a quick breakfast at the counter of the coffee shop in the hotel, then caught a taxi to the hospital.

When Nancy reached the floor Bess was on, the first thing she did was find the duty nurse.

"Bess Marvin, down in two-oh-three? I have good news for you."

"What?" Nancy asked with excitement. "What is it? Is she awake?"

"No," the nurse admitted. "She's not actually awake, not yet. But the night shift girls said that she spoke in her sleep during the night. I know that doesn't seem like much, but it's a very good sign that she'll recover fully. And it probably means that she'll wake up soon."

"That's terrific news," Nancy told the nurse. "Thank you so much."

Encouraged by the progress Bess had made since the day before, Nancy stayed with her friend for the entire morning visiting session, hoping that Bess would regain consciousness while she was there.

Nancy sat beside Bess's bed and remembered all the fun they had had over the years and all the times Bess had helped her with cases. In many ways it seemed odd to her that she was getting ready to look into the murders of Carl Dubchek and Anthony Green without

Bess or George or Ned Nickerson, her boy-friend.

That's the way it has to be this time, she thought.

Bess stirred, making soft noises several times during the two-hour visiting period. Each time Nancy would lean forward, hoping that would be Bess's moment of recovery, but although it was obvious her friend was trying to wake up, she hadn't come to by the time visiting hours were over.

Nancy stood up and took Bess's hand, and as she did, her friend suddenly murmured, "Get them, Nancy."

Shocked, Nancy cried, "Bess! Bess, you're awake!"

Bess's eyes did not open. Nancy suddenly realized that her friend had somehow sensed her presence and even though still unconscious had wished her well.

Nancy smiled, then looked down at her friend and told Bess softly, "I have to go, but don't you worry. I'm going to find out what's going on and get the guys who did this. And then I'm going to take you out for the biggest double chocolate fudge sundae they make in Los Angeles."

After that Nancy held her friend's hand for a long moment. When the nurse opened the door, letting her know that visiting hours were over,

Nancy left quietly, more determined than ever to find the people responsible for her friend's condition.

Nancy studied the surrounding neighborhoods from the window of the taxi she had hailed outside the hospital. She was on her way to the scene of Carl Dubchek's murder. It had not been easy for her to get started. After she had given the address she wanted to the driver, the man tried to refuse to take her. When she had insisted, he relented, but not until he had warned her about her destination.

"That's no kind of place for anyone to go alone," he had said sternly. "It's not even a place for me. What do you want to go there for?"

"I have business there"—she looked at the cab driver's license—"Aldo Santoro. If you don't take me there I'll report you so fast you won't know what happened."

"Fine, fine," the man muttered. "Get in. You want to go that deep into no-man's-land, I'll take you. But you pay me now. I'm not chasing a deadbeat fare through that neighborhood."

Nancy took several bills out of her wallet and handed them to the man. She quickly realized that if the neighborhood was really as bad as the cab driver said it was, then he had a good reason to be suspicious of *anyone* who wanted to go there.

As the taxi got closer to the area, Nancy realized the driver had not exaggerated. And when it seemed that the neighborhood they were going through could not get any seedier, the driver pulled over to the curb.

"Here you go," he said, handing Nancy her change over the seat.

Nancy took the money, handing the man back a couple dollars as a tip as she made her way to the curb. She turned to ask him to wait a few minutes for her, but before she could, the man gunned his engine and made a quick U-turn, driving back the way he had come.

Nancy shouted and waved her arms, but it was no use. The driver was clearly too frightened to wait an extra moment. Deciding to push on, Nancy turned her attention to the reason she was there. She quickly found the right lot, recognizing it from the police photos she had seen the day before.

As she headed down the street toward it, she saw a man in a well-tailored suit enter the lot. Curious, she moved forward more cautiously, careful not to make any noise as she approached.

Nancy crept up on the area and stopped at the edge of the garbage-strewn lot. She scanned the tall weeds for the man she had seen. She found him quickly, and much more. Before she could do anything, she heard the well-dressed man say, "I think he's right, too."

Then she watched as he pulled out a gun and aimed it at Joe Hardy. Her eyes locked with Joe's as the man cocked the hammer of his weapon and demanded, "I'll take that."

Chapter

Ten

H EY, PAL—OKAY, OKAY," Joe answered, his eyes still locked on Nancy's. By this point, Frank had seen Nancy as well. As the gunman drew closer, Joe waved his hands and shouted his words.

"We don't want any trouble."

"Good for you" was all the well-dressed man with the gun had time to say before Nancy struck him from behind. Her elbow hit the small of his back and he went down, startled.

"Nice cover, Joe," Nancy shouted as he and Frank ran forward.

"Hey," Joe answered, "a little shouting to cover the sound of my favorite River Heights resident's footsteps so she can nail a bad guy is the least I can do."

Frank chuckled and shook his head. Only Joe would be making jokes at a time like this, he thought.

Frank moved forward quickly. "I got him!" he shouted. Stepping in close to the man, Frank kicked hard, knocking the man's weapon off into the weeds.

"Thanks, Nancy," Joe said. He gave her a quick hug. "We owe you one."

Before Nancy could say anything, the man rolled over and pulled a knife from the inside of his jacket. Frank was ready, though. He kicked again and his foot hit the man squarely on the chin.

The assailant collapsed onto the ground.

"Nice, Frank," Nancy said. "I hope you didn't hurt him too much."

Joe bent down to check the man's breathing and pulse. "Looks like he'll be sleeping for a while."

"That's why these creeps always lose—they don't take their work seriously enough," Frank said.

"Cut the wisecracks," Nancy said with a chuckle. "Tell me—who is this guy? What's going on? I assume you two are here to investigate the Carl Dubchek murder, correct?"

"Whoa," Frank answered. "Slow down,

Nancy. It's amazing enough seeing you here, but finding out what case we're on is too much!"

"Trust me, Frank," Nancy said, snapping her answer as she thought of Bess lying unconscious in the hospital, "Everything that's happening is too much."

As both Frank and Joe's eyes grew wide with surprise, Nancy added quickly, "I'm sorry, I really am, I'm just on edge because of what happened to Bess."

Nancy filled Frank and Joe in on the events that had brought her to the vacant lot. She recapped the last day and a half for them quickly, starting with Carl Dubchek's murder and ending with her findings at the forensics lab.

Frank did the same for her. Just as fast, he told her about the bamboo truck heist and then gave her a brief rundown of everything he and Joe had gotten off the Internet the night before, finishing with Joe and his brief meeting with Lieutenant Vickler.

"What a coincidence," Joe said. "We all end up contacting the same detective. At least that story about his partner explains why he wouldn't help us."

"That and Bess," Frank added. "How's she doing?"

"No change yet," Nancy answered. "So, I

decided instead of just sitting around in the hospital to be out here doing something."

"I'm really sorry to hear about Bess," Frank said, putting a hand on Nancy's shoulder. "If there's anything we can do to help . . ."

"Yeah," Joe said.

"Thanks, you two," Nancy said. "I'm lucky to have you as friends. It's funny," she added, "but I can't remember ever having to work an investigation by myself before. There's always been someone to help, to bounce ideas off, to just . . . *be* there."

"We're here, Nancy," Frank said. "The three of us will wrap this up in no time."

"And it wouldn't be the first time," Joe said.

"Fine with me," Nancy answered. "Let's get on with it. So, you think this guy is CIA," she said, indicating the man on the ground. "You did know Dubchek was ex-CIA, didn't you?"

"Yes," Joe answered.

"Well," Nancy responded, "that puts you one up on the police."

Joe bent down and rolled the unconscious man over. He went through his pockets. "But just for fun, let's see if we can't get two up on them while we're at it."

In another second Joe had found the man's wallet. "Maybe this will tell us something."

Just as Joe stood up and started to go through

the wallet's contents, the sound of a speeding vehicle caught Frank's attention.

"Something's coming!" he shouted.

All their heads turned as one, just in time to see a small truck coming up over the sidewalk.

"Run!" Frank shouted. "Split up—move!"

Joe and Nancy dodged to the left while Frank threw himself to the right. The truck narrowly missed all of them and the unconscious man.

The three friends stayed low and hidden in the weeds.

"I'll head for the car. Follow me," Frank said.

"We're the only car at the curb," Joe told Nancy. "We'd better give Frank a minute or so head start, then we'll make our way to it. You ready?"

"Say the word," Nancy answered. She could feel the gritty mud of the garbage-filled lot smearing into her jeans as she and Joe crawled for the curb.

Frank kept one eye on the truck as he backed toward the street. He watched as the passenger side of the cab opened and two men wearing baseball caps exited. They scooped up the body of the unconscious man and threw him into the back of the truck. Then each man pulled out a gun and stalked off through the weeds as the truck inched forward.

Time to get out of here, Frank thought. He

headed for the street as quickly as he could without revealing his position. He already had the keys to the car out and clutched in his right hand.

Lucky thing that truck is making so much noise, he thought. We should all be able to get out of here before they find us.

Frank could tell from the sound of the engine that the truck had stopped moving deeper into the lot and had turned around.

Remaining as flat as he could, Frank pushed his way out onto the sidewalk. Reaching the front of the car, Frank took a deep breath and then rolled over the edge of the curb into the street. Just a few more inches . . . almost there now . . .

"Over there!"

Frank sprang up at the sound of the voice coming from the field, thinking he had been spotted. It took him only a second to realize that one gunman had seen Nancy and Joe. He unlocked the door to the car, then shouted, "Run for it!"

Joe and Nancy stood and ran for the car as Frank threw himself inside. In the background Frank could hear the truck moving toward them. Gunfire joined the noise of the truck. In the rearview mirror he could see Joe and Nancy running toward him.

The sound of the truck stopping told them

that it had stopped to pick up the two gunmen. By the time the engine was gunned again, Nancy and Joe had reached the car. Nancy threw herself in the front passenger door, which Frank had standing open.

"Go, go!" Joe screamed as he pushed in alongside Nancy. One of his feet still touched the sidewalk as Frank peeled away from the overgrown lot.

Frank was grateful for the deserted neighborhood. There were few cars or people in sight, and that made it easier for him to break the speed limit without having to worry about an accident.

In his rearview mirror he could see the truck full of gunmen closing on their car. No matter how quick Frank went or how sharply he took the turns, the truck stayed close behind him.

Two bullets whizzed toward the car. One crashed into its trunk, peeling paint and digging a long gouge in the metal of the lid of the trunk. Watching out the back window, Joe shouted, "Man, I'm glad we sprang for the insurance package when we rented this thing."

"We're going to need more than insurance," Frank yelled back. "I'm trying, but I can't seem to shake these guys."

"Who are they, anyway?" Nancy shouted.

Joe opened the wallet he had taken from their first assailant. Now he began to dig through it.

"Any ideas on what these guys want, Nancy?" Joe asked. "Or even who they are, for that matter?"

"Nope," Nancy answered, holding on to the dashboard as Frank took an extremely sharp turn. "But I'll bet they're the same guys who killed Anthony Green and Carl Dubchek."

"Guys," Joe shouted over the noise of the car and the truck following them, "we've got a problem."

"What could possibly be a problem compared to being chased by a truck full of goons with guns?" Frank asked.

"You're not going to believe what this driver's license says. All I can say is, things just got a whole lot weirder."

Joe handed the small plastic-laminated square over to Nancy. "This says that *he* is Carl Dubchek," she shouted. "But that doesn't make sense!"

And then, before anyone could answer, the interior of the car filled with glass as a pair of bullets tore through the rear window.

Chapter

Eleven

T HE SAFETY GLASS in the car's front and rear windshields shattered into pellets. The first two bullets were followed by three more. Glass beads exploded throughout the interior of the vehicle as the spray of bullets passed through from the back to the front. The shells missed Frank, Joe, and Nancy completely.

"That's it," Frank shouted. "I'm getting us out of this—now!"

Frank put on his right turn signal and floored the gas pedal at the same time. The truck behind them speeded up as well.

"Probably want to make sure they have us in range," Joe said, sticking his head up over the front seat, watching the truck behind them through the shattered back window.

"You keep giving them a tempting target," Nancy said, "and they just might check to see if they have it yet."

"Hang on!" Frank ordered.

His turn signal still blinking right, Frank turned left in the hopes of confusing the driver behind him into thinking he was about to pull a trick. Frank could see the truck jerk to the right in his mirror, then jerk back to the left.

The truck shot forward, pursuing Frank into the left turn. With the driver behind him racing forward, Frank continued to turn his wheel, just entering the sidestreet and then making a U-turn and doubling back out of it.

Frank leaned on his horn and drove straight for the truck, then veered off at the last second as the other driver turned his wheel to avoid Frank. The truck hit its brakes, and Frank pushed his car forward at top speed.

He went only a block, then made the first left he came to. He followed that with the next right, the next left, and so on. By the time the truck filled with gunmen had their vehicle back out onto the main street, Frank's zigzagging escape had taken them far from the area.

Nancy looked over at Frank and applauded coolly as if she were at a concert and not running for her life.

"Nice driving," she told him.

Frank smiled faintly, but didn't answer. He was too busy making good their escape.

After getting away from the killers chasing them, Nancy suggested that the first thing they had to do was get a new car.

"She's got a point," Joe said. "Driving without a windshield, or rear window for that matter, *is* against the law."

"I know," Frank said. "Besides, not reporting what happened to the police and the car agency as soon as possible will cause us even more problems. We'd better get things cleared up as soon as we can."

Nancy suggested they contact Lieutenant Vickler since he was in charge of the Dubchek case. The Hardys agreed. Once they reached a better neighborhood, Frank started looking for a pay phone. He pulled over to the curb near a bank of phones in front of Madame Blavatsky's Tarot Reading Parlor.

"Maybe we should just ask Madame Blavatsky what's going on," Joe said.

Nancy frowned and headed for the phones instead. Luckily, she was able to locate Lieutenant Vickler with little trouble. She explained what had happened and gave the detective the details over the phone as briefly as she could, then she asked, "T-Bone, would you meet us at the car rental place? It would help a lot."

"Would I?" the lieutenant answered. "Ms. Drew, I wouldn't miss this for the world."

On the way there, Nancy and the Hardys discussed their cases.

"It's funny," Joe said. "We came at this from such different angles, but it's clear we're working on the same case."

"Yes," Frank added. "The same case as our friend T-Bone."

"Since he's going to meet us at the car agency," Nancy said, "maybe we should agree on just how much we're going to tell Detective Vickler."

By the time they were finished, the list of things Nancy and the Hardys decided to tell T-Bone turned out to be quite short.

The detective moved the necessary paperwork along and got them off the hook for the damages on the first car and got them a new car as well. He also took their reports on the spot and got them back on the street far quicker than they had anticipated.

"Thanks, T-Bone," Nancy said as they all stood together on the sidewalk.

"Yeah," Frank said. "Since the car was rented in my name, I appreciate it a lot."

"Don't sweat it, kid," the big man answered. "Let me just get the facts straight—you and your brother went snooping around the scene of Carl Dubchek's murder, and one guy got the drop on you there. With Nancy's help you escaped, but this first guy and a truckload of other shooters chased you and did all the damage I saw in the garage back there—correct?"

"Yes, sir," Joe said. "That's pretty much what happened."

"But none of you got a good enough look at any of these guys to come downtown and identify them in our photo files. Correct again?"

Nancy nodded. "How about you, Lieutenant? Have you turned up anything new yet?"

The detective seemed a bit startled. He stuck his hands in his pockets. "No. I guess I'm not trying as hard as you kids."

Nancy could tell from the sour look on his face that T-Bone Vickler was neither happy nor satisfied.

The lieutenant turned to leave, then paused. "I'm going to let you kids go because I think doing anything else would be a waste of my time. But I want to tell you that you're playing with fire. I don't know what's going on here, but I do know that it has to be something big."

"I assure you, Detective Vickler," Joe said, "we're not the kind of kids to get mixed up in anything illegal."

"Right," Vickler said. "But you *are* just the kind of kids who think that nothing can hurt them, who think they know it all . . . who end up in the morgue because they thought they knew better than the police how to deal with criminals."

Nancy looked at Joe and Frank and took in a deep breath. She narrowed her eyes, warning them not to respond. She knew it wasn't time to argue with the detective, certainly not while they were still holding the wallet they had taken off the guy in the vacant lot.

"Well," Nancy said once the detective was out of earshot, "I'll admit I feel a little bad about deceiving Vickler, but I'm not about to back off on this one. What about you two?"

"What?" Joe asked. "You thought you were hanging out with some *other* guys named Hardy?"

"That's just what the detective was warning us about," Frank said. "And let's face it, he's more on the money than he knows. This is turning into a pretty big case. We've got guys down in San Diego who nearly run people over just to steal bamboo. They turn out to be connected to people here in Los Angeles who've already killed two men and who tried to kill us. Throw in one of the bad guys walking around with an ID that says he's a dead man—"

"Not to mention the CIA," Nancy added.

"I don't blame Vickler," Joe said. "He had to

say something to try to scare us. He's just doing his job."

"And he's worried about us," Nancy said. "But this case has gotten too personal as far as I'm concerned. I don't know about you two, but I'm not about to turn this one over to the police."

"That's not the way we work, either," Frank said. "But if we're going to keep looking into this, we'd better get serious."

"Way ahead of you, Frank," Joe answered. "Back in the car rental place, I looked through the rest of the wallet when I went to the restroom."

"What did you find?" Frank asked.

"Only one thing that might lead us anywhere. And I emphasize the word *might.*"

Joe slid the wallet out of his back pocket and opened it. He then pulled a piece of folded paper from one of its interior pockets. On it was an address written in pen, looking as if it had been scribbled hurriedly. Frank examined the paper.

"Only one fold—and it's fresh. He hasn't been carrying this around with him a long time, and all the edges are still crisp. This may not actually be a lead, but it's certainly the best thing we have going for us right now."

"Then let's go take a look at wherever this is," Nancy said.

At that moment the rental agent on duty came out to the sidewalk. Nancy studied the expression on his face, as well as the tense way he was holding the set of keys in his hand. It was clear to her that he wasn't happy about having to rent them another car.

Too bad, she thought. We've got things to do.

Frank signed the papers, and in less than a minute, they were on their way.

Nancy and the Hardy brothers were not at all surprised to discover that the address Joe had found in the second Dubchek's wallet was in the same neighborhood where the first Dubchek had been murdered.

"This just gets more interesting all the time," Joe said. "I wonder if Dubchek One and Dubchek Two were twins or something."

Nancy stared at the building before them, answering, "I guess we're about to find out. So, what do we do now?"

"Good question," Frank said. The building they had discovered at the address written on the slip of paper proved to be a warehouse in the neighborhood.

With its boarded and shuttered windows, its doors locked with loosely hung rusting chains, the crumbling three-story structure appeared abandoned at first glance.

A closer look revealed that one of the front doors had been used recently. For one thing, there was no garbage piled in front of it, unlike the other two doors in the warehouse's front wall.

They also noted a drag line in the dirt that indicated the door had been forced through the mud that had built up everywhere else. While Frank and Nancy had spotted those clues, Joe had found fresh tire tracks leading up to the central garage door.

"You know," Joe said, "this is a pretty crummy neighborhood, but the way this dump is set off by itself, no other buildings attached, with open lots on both sides . . ."

"I know what you mean," Frank said. "If I were a crook, this place would appeal to me."

"Only one way to find out if we're right," Nancy said. She began testing the doors one at a time.

While Joe helped her, Frank gave the neighborhood around them a quick scan. He didn't notice anyone watching them. In fact, he didn't notice anyone at all. By the time he'd made certain no one was observing their attempt to break into the warehouse, his brother and Nancy had found their way inside.

One of the other doors was in such a sorry state of deterioration that rather than keeping it closed, the rusting chains strung across it were there to hold it up. It took the three of them only a few seconds to push the door sideways, slip inside, and then replace it.

The interior of the building was almost worse than the outside. Fifty-five-gallon drums of foul-smelling fuel sat close to the entrance. Garbage was piled everywhere, great heaps of it shoved into all the corners. Most of it was paper, ancient packing wads, and decaying cardboard boxes, now all smashed and forgotten and covered with dust.

Nancy tapped one of the metal fuel drums lightly. "What could they have these here for?" she asked the Hardys in a whisper.

"Smells like grease mixed with gas," Frank answered just as quietly. "It could have been used to clean engine parts."

Nancy took another look around the decaying warehouse. "My guess is they're getting ready to burn the place down for the insurance money," she said.

Joe pointed to the light switch near the door. "What do you think?" he asked.

"Better not risk it," Frank said. "It doesn't look like anyone's here, but turning on the lights would be a dead giveaway if anyone comes back before we're done."

Nancy and Joe nodded in agreement. "Besides," Frank added, "there's still enough light in here to see."

"We'd better be careful this place doesn't fall in on us," Nancy said.

As she moved past the Hardys, heading for the rear of the warehouse, Joe chuckled. "I guess these guys aren't the best housekeepers," he said.

"Oh, I don't know," Nancy answered, calling to the Hardys from a point farther back in the warehouse. "They seem to be able to keep some things nice and clean."

The brothers joined her. "But they certainly have an unusual way of going about it," Joe added.

Before them, in the middle of the warehouse's decay and ruin, stood a tall, clean glass chamber. Standing within the glass room were stands of bamboo plants, still in their pots labeled Property of the San Diego Zoo.

"Will you look at that," Joe said.

Frank inspected the chamber, noting the one-foot-square hole cut in its side.

While he tried to determine the purpose of either the chamber or its mysterious opening, Nancy called out to them. "Back here, guys! Come here," she shouted.

What Nancy had found was a blue car.

"What's the big deal?" Joe asked.

"This car—it's the same make and model as the one that was used when they shot up our hotel room and put Bess in the hospital."

"You said that car was red, didn't you?" Joe asked, studying the car.

"True," Nancy said. "But doesn't this paint job look awfully new to you?"

"It sure does," Joe said. "And whoever did it was in a big hurry. The hood is all streaked."

Stepping back from the car, Joe crossed his arms and stared as if trying to make up his mind about something. Then he stepped forward toward the driver's door.

"And you know, if this bad boy was painted in a hurry . . ."

Opening the door on the driver's side, Joe knelt down and inspected its inner locking panel. Smiling, he pointed to a faint rectangular outline on the panel.

As Nancy came closer, he pointed to the rectangle and told her, "See that? That's the inspection sticker. A lot of times guys doing quick repaint jobs will go right over these. So, your first theory holds water. This car was repainted in a hurry. Now, for your second theory . . ."

After pulling out his pocketknife, Joe opened it to the largest blade and began scraping at the edge of the painted-over sticker. Suddenly the corner of the sticker pulled away, revealing a rectangle of red paint.

"I'd say you might be right on the money again, Ms. Drew."

Then, before Nancy could reply or Joe could say anything further, Frank came hurrying toward them, moving as silently as he could. Nancy watched as Frank put a finger to his mouth, warning both her and Joe to remain silent. Then he pointed back toward the entrance to the warehouse.

Suddenly lights were snapped on all around them. As Joe and Nancy listened, they heard what Frank had heard—heavy footsteps and gruff male voices. The voices of four men moving quickly through the warehouse. The voices were getting louder—which meant only one thing.

The men were headed straight for Nancy, Frank, and Joe.

Chapter

Twelve

J OE HEARD THE FOOTSTEPS stop as voices rose in anger. He and his brother and Nancy looked around for an escape route or a hiding place. Every door and window they could see was as tightly sealed as the ones in the front of the warehouse.

Joe tapped Nancy and Frank on the shoulders. When he had their attention, he pointed across the room to a ladder welded to the wall. The ladder led up into the warehouse's rafters. "Up?" Joe mouthed.

"If we can avoid any broken sections," Nancy whispered, "we'll probably be safe."

The trio tiptoed across the warehouse floor toward the ladder.

"Just move it!" A man's voice, angry and demanding thundered from the first floor. Nancy, Frank, and Joe froze in their tracks. "I don't care who did it. The only thing that's important is getting our test run and getting out of here. So let's do it—shall we?"

As Nancy started up the ladder, Joe and Frank looked at each other. Joe was positive the voice belonged to the man who had gotten the drop on him and his brother earlier in the vacant lot, the second Carl Dubchek.

Joe was halfway up the ladder, Frank right behind him when they heard two other voices, voices with Chinese accents. Joe finished climbing and slipped over the edge of a support beam, moving back into the rafters to make room for Frank.

Joe knew better than to risk speaking, so he gave Frank a grin to let him know he thought things were coming together at last. Joe knew Frank understood when his brother nodded his head in agreement.

Then, looking around, Frank mouthed a single word to Joe.

Nancy?

Joe pointed to indicate that Nancy had already moved down the support beam, trying to get closer to the activity below. Frank nodded. Instantly, both he and Joe began to make their way down the old beam in the same direction, moving as quietly as possible.

"All right, all right," Dubchek Two's voice echoed loudly through the warehouse. "Get it in there. But go easy, for pete's sake. Don't drop it."

Nancy pointed down as Joe crawled closer to her position. As he got nearer, he could see what she had noticed. Dubchek Two was standing near the glass chamber. Next to him was another man none of them had ever seen before. Coming up next to Dubchek and the unknown man, two Chinese men were struggling with a large metal box, which they were trying to handle carefully.

Joe breathed a sigh of relief when the old cross-section, which was bearing his and Nancy's weight, held. He looked in the direction Nancy was now pointing. This time Nancy was indicating the two Chinese men.

Joe understood the questioning look on her face and studied the pair closely.

He nodded, indicating that he was certain they were the two men whom he and Frank had tangled with earlier at the zoo in San Diego. As Frank joined his brother and Nancy, Joe pointed out the two men below. Frank silently agreed that they were indeed the bamboo thieves.

Frank lost his balance for a split second, and

his foot slipped. He didn't make any noise, but his shoe peeled back a small layer of dust, sending it drifting toward the floor.

Joe held his breath as he watched the twisting cloud of dust fall toward the floor below. Luckily, none of the men noticed it. Joe wiped his forehead with an exaggerated motion to indicate how dangerous he thought their position was.

The warehouse had a concrete floor, its walls cinder block for only the first four feet. After that the building was constructed from wood—dry, brittle wood, with grease and dust covering every inch.

"Man," Joe whispered, "we came up into the rafters thinking this was the best possible hiding place. Now I'm beginning to have my doubts."

"I know," Frank said, "but it's too late to do much about it now."

"Let's just keep quiet," Nancy said, "stay in the shadows, and hope for the best. Unsafe as it might be here, at least it gives us a good vantage point to see what's going on."

Joe nodded his agreement but put his finger to his lips. The men below had begun talking again, and he wanted to hear every word.

"I think it's in place now," one of the men said. As Joe and the others watched, Dubchek Two moved forward. By this time, two of the men had moved the metal box into the hole that had been cut in the glass room. Joe wasn't surprised when the box fit as perfectly as the last piece in a jigsaw puzzle.

"Well, then," Dubchek said, reaching into his pocket, "I guess the only thing to do is test it."

Dubchek had pulled from his jacket what appeared to be the same type of cylinder that the Hardys had discovered at the crime scene in the vacant lot. Dubchek opened a recessed door in the metal box and inserted the gas cylinder.

Once Dubchek put both his hands inside the box, Joe couldn't see exactly what he was doing. But from the cramped position of his shoulders and the amount of time he was taking, he could tell the man was working with extreme caution.

At the same time the man whom neither Joe nor his companions recognized went over to a cardboard box at the side of the glass chamber. It was a much newer box than the others in the warehouse. Because of the dim light Joe hadn't noticed it earlier. He saw it now, however, his eyes opening wide as the unknown man began to pass out gas masks to his three companions.

"What do we do now?" Joe whispered.

"Keep cool," Frank whispered back. "The glass box is sealed. They're just being careful."

Joe nodded, as did Nancy. Then, as he watched, the men below began to reposition themselves. Dubchek Two and the other two men moved to the side of the glass box affording the clearest view. The unknown man moved in the opposite direction, taking up a new position next to the metal box.

"Mr. Kirby," Dubchek's muffled voice came through his gas mask, "if you think all is ready?"

"We'd better be ready," the man near the metal box growled. "Too much has gone wrong with this operation so far."

"Nothing else will go wrong," Dubchek answered coolly. "I think we all know that."

"I know that you made a lot of promises to me and to everyone here," the man answered. "So far, I'm afraid, not one promise has been kept."

"A strong accusation but essentially true, I admit," Dubchek said. "Now, however, if you would please start the test, let us discover if those days are behind us or not."

"All right," the man Dubchek had called Mr. Kirby snapped. "Here goes."

Even through their masks, the two men's words had been understandable to Joe. Having heard the conversation between those below him, Joe was not prepared for what happened next.

As Kirby manipulated a control within the

metal box, a thin spray shot forward into the glass chamber from the metal box. Within seconds, the entire glass room began to fill with a slight purplish hue. The colored tinge blurred the bamboo within but never hid it entirely. Then, after only another few seconds, the purple haze began to fade.

"This is it," one of the men said as he and his companion began to move forward. Dubchek said, "Stay still. Don't block the view. We all want to see."

You can say that again, Joe thought, staring down at the glass chamber. What could those guys be up to? he silently asked.

Joe Hardy got his answer.

"Look," Kirby shouted, pointing to the upper leaves of the bamboo. "Look! It's started. It's working!"

From his vantage point, Joe couldn't see anything that appeared much different in the glass chamber.

What's started? he wondered. What's working?

Staring as hard as he could and leaning forward precariously, Joe strained to make sense of the bizarre scene below. Then it happened. . . .

"Uh-oh," he muttered.

So startled was he that Joe actually spoke

above a whisper. He noticed that neither Nancy nor Frank chastised him for it, though. He was certain they were as shocked as he was by what was happening inside the chamber.

"Look—it's advancing," one of the men said. "Watch, you can see it moving right down the leaves, down the stems. . . ."

"I got eyes," Kirby growled. "I can see."

So can I, Joe thought, although he was certain he was a great deal more disturbed by what he could see than Mr. Kirby was.

The bamboo within the glass chamber was dying. Although the contents of the cylinder had been emptied into the clear room less than two minutes earlier, the bamboo inside was already almost completely destroyed.

"Well, this is it, men," Dubchek Two said, his mood suddenly much sunnier. "This is what we wanted."

"You didn't believe it would work," Kirby sneered. "But I told you. I told you it had been pretested, that it was all there, just waiting for us to grab it."

What? Joe wondered. Tested by whom? Waiting where? What are you up to? You're going through all of this just to destroy bamboo? What kind of good is that going to do for you?

Joe pushed aside his questions for the moment to study the effects below. He had been timing events with the second hand of his watch, trying his best to memorize the stages of destruction.

At sixty seconds results were already noticeable. At ninety seconds the upper leaves were dropping off. At one hundred and twenty the upper stems were wilting, turning black, curling up. At one hundred and eighty the main stalks of the bamboo were black, shriveled.

Then suddenly Joe realized there was no point in memorizing the speed of the effects. All he had to remember was that within two minutes every bit of green within the glass chamber had been destroyed.

"I don't get it," Joe whispered to his brother. "Who would want to destroy bamboo so bad they'd risk killing people to prove they could do it?"

"Those guys haven't just *risked* killing," Nancy added in a hushed tone. "They've killed people, and they've tried to kill us and Bess."

Frank said nothing, putting up a hand to indicate that they had all better stop talking before one of them was overheard.

"All right, gentlemen," Dubchek said. "We've done what we needed to. Is everything in the van?"

"What isn't packed is right here," Kirby answered, indicating several small boxes next to the one from which he had pulled the gas masks earlier.

"Good," Dubchek said. "If it wouldn't be beneath the dignity of members of the Kwau Kuai to help Mr. Kirby move a few boxes . . ."

"The Kwau Kuai," Frank whispered. "That's the street name for the old Chinese Communist secret police."

Below, the four men busied themselves gathering together the few boxes they planned to remove from the warehouse. Then, as they headed for the door, Dubchek said, "We haven't quite kept to our original schedule or plan—"

"Thanks to those interfering children," one of the Kwau Kuai agents snapped.

"Now, now, Lun," Dubchek answered the man, "let's not worry about that now. Finally everything seems to be back on schedule. The only thing we need to worry about is destroying the evidence."

As he spoke, Dubchek pushed over one of the large drums of fuel near the door. Waiting until the others had passed through to the outside, he knocked over a second drum as well.

"Frank, Joe," Nancy whispered. "Weren't those things filled with oil or gas or something?"

"Let's get out of here," Frank answered.

Closest to the ladder, he turned and headed back in the direction from which they'd come.

He'd managed to crawl only three feet when the floor below burst into an inferno of flame and smoke.

They were trapped in the warehouse with no hope of escape.

Chapter

Thirteen

 MOVE, FRANK, MOVE!" Nancy shouted.

Thick, dark smoke was filling every corner of the warehouse, causing Nancy and the Hardys to cough and choke. Waves of flame tore across the floor, gliding along the sea of spilled fuel, igniting everything within the tinderbox of a building.

"Wait," Nancy cried. Pointing below, she shouted to the others, "It's no use going back the way we came. We can't go down the ladder."

"You're right," Frank answered. "The whole floor is already covered in fire!"

"What can we do?" Joe asked. Covering his mouth with his sleeve, desperately trying to keep the rising smoke out of his lungs, he added, "We're trapped."

"Not yet!" Nancy cried. Blinking against the harsh smoke stinging her eyes, she pointed off toward the far wall. "Do you see where the smoke is going?"

"Up," Joe replied, "but it's not collecting on the ceiling."

"Right," Frank said. "It's getting out through those holes in the roof."

"Well, gang," Nancy said, fighting the urge to cough as the smoke filled her lungs, "if it can get out that way, so can we!"

Nancy led the way, moving across the beam toward the closest hole. The heat lapped its way up the walls, devouring the dry cardboard and other piles of junk. Old canisters of oil and chemicals went up, adding a deadly ooze to the already choking smoke.

Keeping an arm across her face, Nancy took short breaths through the fabric of her clothes, filtering as much of the smoke as she could. She moved slowly, cautiously, unable to see her feet below or her hands in front of her. Then, suddenly—

"Nancy!"

Nancy gasped at the sound of Frank's voice. She turned in time to see his feet slip from the rafter. He managed to catch hold of the rotting beam with one hand, desperately clawing for a hold with the other.

"Frank!" Joe shouted as an updraft suddenly blew smoke in his and Nancy's faces. "Where are you?"

"Here," Frank gasped. Then a moment of luck was granted to Nancy and her companions as the fire below found a new source. Reaching another large stand of old boxes, the flames pushed away the billowing smoke for the moment. Nancy could see Frank once more as he worked feverishly to regain a second handhold on the beam.

Nancy waited while Joe moved back past his brother. Then, working as carefully as they could, Joe and Nancy pulled on Frank as hard as they could without sending themselves over the edge.

Finally Frank managed to get a knee back up over the crossbeam. As he pulled himself into a sitting position, Nancy edged over to him. "Frank, can you move—can you make it?"

"Yes," Frank answered, his voice harsh from the amount of smoke he had inhaled. "Don't worry about me. Let's just get out of here!"

Nancy turned back and continued to work her way across the narrow beam toward the hole in the roof. Flames leaped up toward them, sparks dancing through the air. A few landed on their clothing and in their hair. It was all they could do to brush the sparks away.

Several sections of the roof were already beginning to smoulder by the time Nancy reached the only hole close to the rafter on which she and the Hardys were. Nancy reached upward, straining her arm as far as she could.

"I can't reach it!" Nancy cried.

"Even if you could," Joe said, pointing at the jagged edge of the hole, "you'd tear yourself on those splinters. Here—hold on. I'll boost you up."

Joe bent down and took a deep breath through his sleeve. Then he wrapped his arms around Nancy's shins and managed to lift her off the narrow beam without loosing his grip or his balance. Joe gritted his teeth and moved as carefully as he could. Seconds later Nancy's head disappeared above the line of the rooftop.

Reaching out, she managed to grab hold of a solid section of the roof. As Joe continued to push her upward, she yelled down to him.

"Let go, Joe! I can get myself out from here."

Nancy coughed as the thick smoke began to billow around her and the Hardys. She maintained her hold as Joe released his grip on her, but her skin was torn by the jagged hole. Nancy ignored the pain and pulled herself up and out of the hole, coughing and gasping for air.

Her first instinct was to get away from the

fumes as quickly as possible, but she couldn't. Taking several quick breaths to clear her lungs, she shouted down through the hole.

"Joe! Take my hand!"

Then she plunged her upper body back into the acrid funnel of smoke pouring out through the hole in the roof. She felt around for Joe's hand in the dark, fearing that she had somehow lost the Hardys.

Finally a hand slapped against hers in the darkness. As she braced herself, Nancy felt a pull, and then suddenly Joe's head popped out of the hole. She pulled with all her strength, surprised that he made it up so easily. Joe coughed for a moment and cleared his lungs, then turned back to help his brother.

"Frank boosted me up," he told Nancy as the two of them groped for him. "We've got to pull him out."

"I've got a hand!" Nancy shouted.

Joe rolled over to Nancy, adding his strength to hers. Just as Frank managed to get his free hand on the edge of the roof, the rushing black smoke suddenly turned a grayish white.

"Pull!" Frank ordered. "The fire just hit the rafter. It's all around me."

Joe and Nancy were dragged across the roof as Frank's weight suddenly seemed to triple.

"The rafter's gone. Hurry!" Frank's voice was urgent.

"I got you, Frank!" Joe screamed. Digging his knees into the crumbling roof, he yanked savagely.

Joe jerked upward, pulling Frank halfway out of the hole and throwing Nancy off balance at the same time. Frank slammed down on the roof, face and chest crashing against the melting tar. Quickly, he jerked himself up out of the hole, dozens of splinters of all sizes breaking off in his abdomen and legs.

Then Nancy could feel the roof splitting under their combined weight. "Separate!" she shouted.

The Hardy brothers threw themselves in one direction, Nancy in another. Nancy gazed across the cave-in, relieved to see that her companions had survived as well. At the same time, flame blasted its way up through the newly expanded opening, spreading across the roof at an alarming rate.

Nancy gasped down great lungfuls of air. As she recovered, the Hardys made their way around the hole to join her at the edge of the building.

"We have to get off this thing *now*," Nancy shouted.

"She's right," Joe said. "The fire's eating away at the roof. This place doesn't have more than a few minutes before it all caves in."

As if to emphasize Joe's point, one of the

back corners of the building collapsed. A great cloud of sparks was thrown into the air along with another massive release of black smoke.

"It's a freestanding building," Nancy said. "There aren't any roofs to jump to. Nothing but concrete—except right over there. . . ."

"It was overgrown on that side," Frank said. "The shrubs might break our fall."

Running toward that side of the roof, Joe shouted to the others, "There's only one way to find out!"

Nancy watched as Joe reached the edge and threw himself forward. She couldn't see what happened to him, but she knew there was no other way to escape the burning roof.

Nancy leaped forward and fell toward the ground three stories below.

"And that's all of it, Lieutenant," Nancy said.

"You kids sure tell one wild story."

Detective T-Bone Vickler stood over Nancy and the Hardys, his arms folded across his chest. Nancy didn't think he looked very happy.

Fire trucks arrived on the scene of the burning warehouse ten minutes after the three investigators had thrown themselves to the ground. When the firefighters and other emergency workers arrived, they found three bruised but happy survivors waiting for them. Landing in the stand of weak-limbed bushes that were in the abandoned lot, Nancy and her companions hadn't broken or even sprained anything.

The ambulances that followed the fire trucks treated Nancy and the Hardys for smoke inhalation, cleaned the cuts they had sustained on the edge of the hole, and taken care of Frank's burns. Then the police had taken them into custody under suspicion of arson.

"So, tell me, are you sure you haven't left anything out?" T-Bone asked. "I mean, this is pretty fascinating stuff—CIA agents, bamboo thieves, drive-by shootings, car chases, sinister gas canisters, and glass chambers. Sure you didn't just show up in L.A. to try to sell a screenplay?"

"Look, Lieutenant," Nancy said, "I know you have all the reason in the world to be upset with us, but when we talked to you before, we didn't realize how big this case was."

"I've made calls to your hometown police departments," Vickler said. "You're all good at detecting, which is why I'm not going to give you any trouble—that is, if you start cooperating with me now."

Smiling, Nancy said, "I think that could be arranged. What do you think, guys?"

"Fine with us, Lieutenant," Joe said. He pointed to his brother's bandaged arm and chest and added, "I could use a new partner.

My brother here can't be trusted with matches anymore."

"You see what I have to work with," Frank answered, rolling his eyes. "I ask you, officer, should anyone have to put up with a guy like this?"

"Okay, okay." T-Bone laughed. "Can the comedy and let's get down to business. Now, I don't think there's much more we can do tonight. Forensics is digging through the remains of the warehouse to see what they can find of this glass room of yours. If there's any trace of this gas machine, they'll find it."

"Sounds good to me," Joe said.

"Normally," Vickler continued, "my guess would be that there isn't a whole lot more we could do tonight. But before I send you three troublemakers back to your hotels, I was wondering what you thought about the murder subject."

"Well," Nancy said, "now that you mention it . . ."

Fifteen minutes later Lieutenant Vickler escorted Nancy and the Hardys into the morgue where Carl Dubchek's body had been since the day before. The lieutenant took Nancy and her companions directly to the area where Dubchek's body had been taken once the police forensic team had finished with it. As they entered, the attendant on duty stepped in their way to stop them.

"Vickler," he asked, "what's the idea of bringing in so many unauthorized people?"

"Calm down," the lieutenant answered. "I've got a crime to solve here, if you don't mind."

The attendant made a few more small complaints but did leave T-Bone alone with the Hardys and Nancy to do as they pleased.

The lieutenant pulled open the drawer containing the body of Carl Dubchek.

"Yup," Vickler said, staring down at the body on the slab, "That's him. That's the Carl Dubchek we scraped up off the street."

"He's the one I heard at the conference," Nancy said. "But still, something has to be wrong here."

"Like what?" Joe asked. "If he's the guy, he's the guy. Right?"

"Maybe not," Nancy said. As everyone turned to stare at her, Nancy added, "T-Bone, did you check this body's fingerprints?"

"No," the lieutenant said. "We didn't need to. Mrs. Grunderson made a positive identification, same as you just did."

The big detective stroked his chin for a moment. "Still, we had no reason to doubt it was Dubchek until now."

Within minutes, Vickler had a uniformed

officer in the morgue, taking the dead man's fingerprints.

"Get those transmitted to Washington—pronto," he ordered. "Tell them we've got big trouble. Run it through the Justice Department. I want to know who this guy is in ten minutes."

Eight minutes later the officer returned with a sheet of fax paper. Nancy watched as Vickler scanned the single sheet.

"Well," she asked impatiently, "was he with the CIA? Is he Carl Dubchek?"

"Oh, he was CIA, all right," the lieutenant responded. "But I don't care what the United Nations conference thinks. The United States government says that man in the drawer is not Carl Dubchek!"

Chapter

Fourteen

"BESS, YOU'RE AWAKE!"

Frank watched Nancy rush to the side of her friend's bed. As he and Joe entered the hospital room behind her, Nancy asked, "How long have you, I mean—when did you regain consciousness?"

"Just a little while ago," Bess answered in a weak voice. "But I feel a lot better already."

"Say, she doesn't look so bad," Joe joked. "I thought you said she was all banged up. Come on, get out of bed, Bess. We've got a killer case this time and we need all the help we can get."

"Oh, Nancy," Bess groaned. "Did you have to bring these two clowns with you?"

"Hey," Frank protested, his hands held up. "What did I do?"

"Well, okay," Bess relented. "I always thought you were okay, Frank, but put a leash on that brother of yours," she added.

"Would that I could," Frank said. "Oh, don't I wish."

Bess smiled gently, then quickly closed her eyes hard, squinting as if she were in pain.

"Are you all right?" Nancy asked. "What's wrong, Bess?"

"I'm okay," Bess answered weakly. "I'm just tired. They said I was unconscious for a long time."

"Only a day or so," Nancy told her friend quietly. "Long enough to scare me pretty well, though."

"Believe me," Bess said, "I'll try to make sure it never happens again."

"How about your parents?" Frank asked. "Do they know you're all right?"

"Yes," Bess answered. "The nurse told me Nancy gave the hospital all the information they needed to keep in touch with my parents. I talked to them this morning."

Frank nodded. Before he could say anything else, Bess turned to Nancy. "What happened to Anthony?"

"He didn't make it, Bess," Nancy told her friend.

"I know that," Bess said, tears filling her eyes. "The doctor told me. But what I meant was, was he involved with something bad? Did he just use me?"

"Bess, we don't know anything for certain yet," Nancy answered. "This has ballooned into a big case. But I can tell you, from what I heard of his conversation on the phone in the restaurant and from what he said to us in the hotel, he wasn't using you. He liked you. A lot. If anything, I believe he was trying to protect you."

Frank said nothing as Nancy moved closer to her friend's bed to hold her hand. He knew they should get moving, that they had an important case waiting for them. But he also knew spending time with Bess was important.

The day nurse entered the room. "I'm afraid I'm going to have to ask you to leave," she announced. "Ms. Marvin needs her rest. She's not ready for this much excitement."

Nancy, Frank, and Joe all said quick goodbyes and headed for the door under the watchful eye of the nurse.

Just as he was to join Nancy and Frank in the hall, Joe turned and asked, "So, Bess, how're the desserts in this place?"

Joe laughed and ducked only a second before the pillow Bess tossed at him bounced off the wall on the opposite side of the hall.

"Good arm on that girl," Frank observed. "I mean, for being in a sickbed."

"Yes," Joe said. "I wonder if she's ever thought about turning pro for the majors."

"I don't think so," Nancy said. "But I am glad to see she's bouncing back from the shock of Anthony's death."

Frank, Nancy, and Joe returned to their car and headed for what seemed to be their best lead.

"So, Frank, you figure we'll actually find this guy at home?" Joe asked.

"It's worth a try," his brother answered. Nancy studied the Los Angeles map and directed Frank as they continued on. "I mean, since the man in the morgue wasn't the real Carl Dubchek, then it stands to reason that the real Carl Dubchek isn't dead. And if he isn't dead, and he isn't at the conference, either, he has to be somewhere."

Frank followed Nancy's directions and made a left turn. She let the Hardys know that they were now on the street where the "real" Carl Dubchek's house was supposed to be. Frank watched for the house number. "But wouldn't the police already have covered his house when they thought he was murdered?" Frank asked.

"That's what I thought last night when we were in the morgue. It didn't dawn on me until this morning when I got up that if the police had a phony Dubchek, that he might have come with a complete set of fake ID."

"Just like the Dubchek whose wallet we took," Joe offered.

"Exactly," Nancy answered. "Since that Dubchek's identification matched him and not the Carl Dubchek whom I heard speak, it stands to reason that the other Dubchek's ID would have given the police a totally different set of clues to work from."

"Makes sense," Frank said, "that the fake Dubchek's wallet had a completely different set of identification from the stuff Nancy was able to get from the convention. Whoever it is we're up against here, they're certainly thorough."

"If the real Dubchek is still alive," Joe challenged, "why did he disappear when the guy we have in the morgue was shot?"

"Good question," Nancy said. As Frank pulled the car over to the corner, Nancy pointed to a man working in his garden. She undid her seat belt. "Why don't we ask him."

Five minutes later Frank, Joe, and Nancy were in the living room of Mr. Carl Dubchek.

Once he had heard their entire story, he said, "I'm sorry if I've caused anyone grief, but I didn't know what else to do. Maybe it was spending too many years with the CIA, but when I heard the reports of my death on the TV, I suppose you could say I panicked."

Frank watched the man as he rose from his chair. He seemed shaken. Before Frank could ask, the man said, "One of my old associates from the CIA had asked if someone could take my place at the conference. We thought there wouldn't be anyone there who knew me. My associate said . . . what he said was probably a lie, wasn't it? Anyway, as long as the world thought I was dead, I decided to let it keep thinking that for a few days while I tried to find out what had happened."

"No offense meant here," Joe said, "but you didn't seem too involved with looking into your so-called murder when we got here."

Dubchek stared at Joe for a moment. Dubchek suddenly looked sad and worn and tired. "Some of what I've found out has been disturbing. I needed to think. Gardening helps me do that."

Dubchek sat back in his chair and stared into space. After a second he rose from his seat. "If you will excuse me for a moment, I'd like to go to my study. If you could remain here, I just need a moment alone."

"Sure thing," Frank answered. Dubchek nodded with gratitude and left the room, moving slowly.

Once he was gone, Joe turned to the others. "You sure he's not going to pull a fast one on us?" he asked.

"I guess we can't be sure of anything in this business," Frank answered, "but he seems okay. And besides, we don't really have any reason to suspect him, do we?"

"No," Nancy answered. "Not yet, anyway. And he is the real Carl Dubchek. Now that we've found him we can finally start getting some answers instead of more questions—I hope."

Then, before either of the Hardys could answer their friend, Mr. Dubchek came back into the room.

"I'm sorry," he said. "But I just had to be alone for a minute. I had to consider . . . what it was I had to offer . . . whether or not I should share it with you."

"I'm sorry, sir," Frank said, "but I'm afraid I don't understand."

"No," Dubchek answered. "I'm certain you don't. But you will. Please—all of you—follow me."

The older man led Frank, Joe, and Nancy to his study. Seating himself at the computer on a large desk covered with books and papers, he turned on the power and began working his way through various start-up screens. "I thought about telling you nothing because I was embarrassed. Ashamed, really, of my part in what I think has come back to haunt me."

Reaching into a side drawer of his desk, Mr. Dubchek fumbled around until he found a 3¼-inch floppy disk. Pulling it free, he held it up, showing it to the trio.

"I haven't touched this disk since 1978," he told them, "not since the whole horrible business was put aside. I thought—hoped, anyway—that I'd never have to see it again. You'd think after all these years with the CIA that I'd know better."

"What is it, sir?" Frank asked.

"It is the outline of a plan—a plan to start a war. It was never used because it was decided it was much too evil to contemplate. I guess it must not be so anymore."

Pushing the disk into his computer, the older man went through a series of passwords to open the first of the files.

"In the late seventies," he said, "we were still terrified of the Communists. Maybe it's hard for kids as young as you to remember, but the world was convinced there would be a nuclear war—and that it would happen the day the Russians and the Chinese joined forces. For those of us who specialized in the study of those cultures, coming up with ways to keep them at each other's throats was our top priority."

Mr. Dubchek pointed to the screen, bringing up an image that Nancy, Frank, and Joe recognized immediately.

"That's one of those gas cylinders," Frank said. "The ones that destroyed the bamboo."

"Yes," said the older man. "But only one specific type of bamboo."

"The type that pandas eat," Joe offered.

"Correct," Dubchek said. Staring at the image on the screen, his voice grew quieter as he explained, "The Chinese love their pandas. The animals are considered national treasures. It's ironic, considering how close they came to dying out."

"I don't understand," Nancy said.

"Oh, I suppose I'm getting off the point. It's just that pandas migrate. They follow the bamboo crop during the growing season. After the pandas would leave a region, farmers moved in and cultivated the land the bears had just stripped clean. Then, when the pandas came back during the next season, there wouldn't be any bamboo for them. As pandas became international stars, the Chinese government began taking measures to protect their habitats."

"But what about the gas?" Frank asked. "What good would it do to destroy all the bamboo in China? It wouldn't kill the pandas. They may eat a lot of it, but I've seen pictures of them eating other things."

"It's true," the older man answered. "But the idea was to release the gas on the Chinese mainland, framing the Russians for the job. It would have thoroughly poisoned relations between the two Communist blocs."

"That's horrible," Nancy said.

"Yes," Dubchek said. "Isn't it? Eventually the bears would have been saved, but it was estimated—let me see . . ."

Dubchek paged through several screens of information before he found the data he was looking for.

"Here it is," he said. " 'Sixty-five to seventy percent of the current panda population would be killed.' Those were the figures."

"What stopped it?" Frank asked. "Why wasn't the plan ever used?"

"Oh, you have to understand, scores of such plans were created. And a lot of them *were* used. But this one . . . well, not only was it extreme, but remember—it was 1978. It wasn't long after that the Russian government began to crumble on its own. We just weren't worried anymore. So, the plan was shelved. Mercifully."

No one spoke. As Mr. Dubchek closed down his computer, Nancy and the Hardys simply stared at the older man, each wondering how such "plans" could be created in the first place.

As Dubchek switched off his machine, Joe spoke up. "I still don't get it. This plan was canceled in 1978. That was a long time ago. And as far as I know, no one is worried about the Russian and Chinese Communists getting together anymore."

"That's true," Nancy said. "If anything, they're both turning capitalist as fast as they can."

"Which leaves a question," Frank said. "If the plan no longer makes sense, why would anyone be thinking of using it?"

"That's a very good question, young man."

Frank turned, as did Joe and Nancy and Mr. Dubchek, at the sound of the voice behind them. So shocked had he, Joe, and Nancy been over the decades-old CIA plan that they hadn't heard anyone enter Dubchek's house.

"A very good question, indeed," the man they had come to know as Dubchek Two said. Frank watched as the man, Kirby, and the two Chinese thieves entered the room.

Then Dubchek Two pointed a heavy .45 caliber automatic at the quartet in the study, a weapon exactly like the ones held by all his companions. "Please," he added, pointing the gun directly between Frank's eyes, "allow me to answer it."

Chapter
Fifteen

NANCY HELD BACK as Frank and Joe moved toward the intruders. Neither was able to take more than a step or two when the rest of the intruders cocked their weapons and leveled them at the Hardys.

Dubchek Two smiled. He continued to hold his own weapon on Frank as he said softly, "You won't make it."

Nancy breathed a sigh of relief when Frank stopped. Nancy stared at Dubchek Two and the others, and the ringleader returned her gaze.

"Ah, that's so much better," he said. "And now, if we could all stand, please?"

Nancy and Mr. Dubchek rose from their seats. The ringleader nodded to them.

"Splendid," he said. "If you keep cooperating, you might finally learn everything you've been trying to piece together on your own."

"You're just going to tell us," Joe snapped. "Is that it?"

"Why not?" Dubchek Two asked. "Your friend here could have cleared up a lot more of this for you if he had really wanted to."

"That's right, Carl," Kirby said. "You could have."

"You traitor," Dubchek answered coldly. "You got me into this because I trusted you. But don't worry. I've told them the important pieces."

Dubchek Two laughed and waved his gun. He first motioned for the Hardys to move back toward Nancy and Dubchek, and then for them all to move away from the computer. After they did, he crossed the room and took the disk from the computer.

He held it up and read its label. Then he smiled. Again Dubchek Two used his gun to indicate that Nancy, Frank, Joe, and Dubchek should move—this time back to the living room. As everyone began to cross the room, careful not to startle any of the gunmen, Dubchek Two finally answered the real Dubchek's statement.

"Oh, Carl, you are much too modest. For instance, did you bother to explain why these young people have run into so *many* Carl Dubcheks?"

"I would have," Dubchek answered coldly. "I thought other things to be more important."

Nancy listened while keeping an eye on the gunmen. As the Hardys moved into the living room, the two Chinese men kept their weapons trained on the brothers. Kirby covered Nancy with the same unblinking efficiency. The ringleader kept his gun on Dubchek, needlessly poking him with its barrel every few seconds as they made their way into the main room.

"You hear that, Kirby?" Dubchek Two said, setting down the oversize tote bag he was carrying. "We are unnoteworthy. The world is filled with things more important than us."

"So," Joe snarled, "you're such a big shot—you tell us."

"But of course," the ringleader said. "It is no great mystery. We are all of us Dubchek."

Nancy and the Hardys stared, not quite understanding what Dubchek Two meant. Realizing that was the case, the real Carl Dubchek explained.

"In the CIA, when any new operation is being tested, everyone is given an identical ID packet. This is so they may access the same information, enter the same secure areas, et cetera. In other words, until phony movement papers are needed, everyone connected to a project is identified by the operation creator's name . . ."

"That means," Nancy said, "that you came up with the idea of destroying bamboo and starving the pandas."

"I'm afraid you're correct," Mr. Dubchek said.

The ringleader laughed at Dubchek's embarrassment. "How delightful. How touching. You are too droll, Carl."

"And you, Cinder, are a monster."

"Cinder!" Nancy exclaimed. "You're the one who had Anthony Green murdered. You're the one who tried to kill me and Bess!"

"So pleased you enjoyed my handiwork," Cinder answered. "Chen, Lun—find something to tie up this bunch with. We need to get this over with once and for all."

With Kirby covering the Hardys, Cinder kept his weapon trained on Nancy and Dubchek. Nancy noted that Joe tried to make a small move, testing Kirby's reflexes. The CIA man spotted the motion instantly, however.

"Don't be stupid, kid. It wouldn't be good for your general well-being."

Seconds later Lun and Chen returned with a

ball of heavy-gauge twine from Dubchek's gardening supplies. Pulling a folding knife from his pocket, the older of the two thugs began cutting free sections of the twine while the other began using it on Frank's wrists, binding them behind his back. The raw strands tore into his skin, but Frank did not complain.

"Don't tell me these two have been going around passing themselves off as Carl Dubchek," Frank said.

"No, Chen and Lun are colleagues of ours, but they are not CIA. They're members of China's famous Gaun Cee Qui."

"What?" Dubchek sputtered. "You're working with the Vampire League?"

"I don't think he likes us." Chen laughed as he cut another length of twine so that his partner could begin tying Frank's ankles.

"I don't think I really care," Lun answered. As the two men finished binding Frank and then started on Joe, Cinder spoke to his old colleague. "It's all perfectly simple, Carl. You created a brilliant plan years ago. For a while there was no need for it. Now there is. So we four have decided to put it into effect."

"But it doesn't make any sense," Dubchek said. "The Soviet Union has fallen apart. China is more open now. What would be the point in employing the plan now?"

"You've been retired too long, Carl," Cinder said with exaggerated sympathy. "You've started believing what you read in the papers. The hard-liners in the Soviet Union are taking control again. Within the next few years, they will be as powerful as they ever were."

"They've traded political espionage for industrial," Kirby offered. "It won't be long before they're as big a problem as they ever were. Bigger, actually, since we've fallen in with them."

Nancy noted that Lun worked carefully, binding Joe's wrists and ankles tightly. He didn't seem to trust either of the Hardys very much, but it seemed to Nancy that he especially disliked Joe.

"China does not need to become entangled with the Russians," Lun said. "My partner and I, we don't have a use for anyone in this room. That's all right. Cinder and Kirby don't like us much either. Am I correct?"

"The only good commie's a dead commie," Kirby answered. Although he laughed as he said it, Nancy could tell he meant what he had said.

"You see?" Lun asked. "The truth is, we are using each other to reach a common goal. The American government has grown weak. In China, it is the same. Our leaders are more interested in profits than the people. But that will change soon."

"Very soon," Chen added.

Nancy watched as Lun finished his work on Joe's ankles. The thug tested the twine, then pulled it tighter. When he seemed satisfied that neither of the Hardys could escape, he took another length of twine from his partner and turned toward Nancy with it.

"It's all quite simple, really," Kirby announced. He appeared to relax somewhat once both the Hardys had been securely bound. Kirby said, "Don't blame the CIA, though. This is all our idea."

"*Your* idea?" Dubchek gasped. "What do you mean?"

"Oh, please, Carl," Cinder answered. "Don't embarrass yourself. Let me make it easy for you. First we gave you a protégé, Anthony Green, to get the sample gas cylinders we knew you'd still have."

"You planted him here?" Dubchek asked.

"Of course. Kirby told you the CIA needed to replace you at the conference. I knew you wouldn't trust me. We asked you to stay home and had Bickner take your place."

"Bickner?" Nancy asked. "Who is Bickner?"

"He was another of the Dubchek squad," Kirby answered. "But he was expendable."

"His job at the conference was to drop hints in the right places about the Russians preparing to do some terrible environmental thing," Cinder said. "Poor Bicky, he never guessed that the easiest way to make his hints seem real was to have him murdered after he uttered them. After we unleash our disaster, people will begin to remember what the murdered lawyer from the convention had hinted at. Calls will be made, fingers will be pointed, the Russians will be implicated, and we will have what we want."

"But what did Anthony Green have to do with your plan?" Nancy asked.

"Why," Cinder answered, "he approached Dubchek, asking for an apprentice's position. Carl was all too happy to take him in. Young Mr. Green was able to gain Carl's trust quickly and then find the gas cylinders even more quickly."

"But then he went soft on us over some girl," Kirby growled. "He refused to get the file disk with the specs—"

"Which has, of course, been taken care of now," Cinder added, patting his pocket, which contained the CIA files on the sinister bamboo destruction operation.

"Yes," Kirby said. He stared at Nancy. "Anyway, we eliminated him, never knowing it would bring the bunch of you into the picture.

But to make the story short, we've tested the gas, which was never done in the old days. It works quite well. And now that we have the files of the operation, we have the formula and will be able to make all we need."

"This doesn't make any sense," Nancy protested. "Why are you doing this?"

"You do not understand?" Lun asked as he finished binding Nancy's ankles. "It is simple. Cinder and Kirby do not trust the Russians. They want your country to remain superior to them. They fear a Soviet-Chinese alliance will throw off the world's balance of power. They think that the Russians will attempt to leech China's newfound strength."

"And," Chen added, "so do we. There are still too many within the regime in Beijing. It is all too possible they could be willing to put aside China's new prosperity for another disastrous union with the Soviets."

"In other words, children," Cinder said, "to make it simple—none of us likes or trusts the Russians, and this is the simplest way we can see to foil their chances at becoming players in the big game."

Nancy did not answer. Instead, she kept her eyes on Lun. He had just finished securing her bonds. Now the thug cut another piece of twine to begin tying Dubchek. She noted Lun cut only one long piece to secure Dubchek

153

but had used two or three on her and the Hardys.

Why would he do things differently just for Dubchek, she wondered.

"What could be easier, kiddies?" Kirby asked. "I mean, when we're finished, the Russians will be discredited. The world will distrust them as never before. The Chinese will hate them. The United States will maintain its leading position of power in the world. The playing field will be level between us and the Chinese as the two major powers in the world, and all it takes is killing a few stupid bears. What could be easier?"

"You're talking about destroying an entire species!" Nancy shouted.

"Oh, lighten up," Cinder groaned. "They won't all die. But once the truth comes out, in other words, once we've framed the Russians, there'll be no chance of them making any kind of deals with the Chinese. They'll be too busy guarding their mutual border."

"I won't say I can't believe this of you, Cinder," Dubchek said. Wincing as Lun wrapped a length of twine around his wrists, Dubchek blinked as if in great pain. "But still— isn't there some appeal that could be made— you act as if this is all so clean and simple, but you know as well as I do that the models were run and run again. The main reason the operation was never put into effect . . . you *know* the risks!"

"That my government will start a war over something like this?" Chen answered. "Those are twenty-year-old predictions. Times change."

Reaching out, the Chinese secret agent of the notorious Gaun Cee Qui, the Vampire League, patted Dubchek on the cheek. "Not to worry, old man. Everything's going to work just the way we say it will," he said in a snide voice.

"It's still unbelievable to me," Nancy said, "that you could consider killing so many endangered animals for such a stupid end."

"Why not?" Kirby answered. "After all, we're willing to kill all of you."

Then the CIA agent crossed the room to the tote bag Cinder had set down earlier. Pulling it open, he slid the sides of it down to reveal its contents—a very nasty-looking gray cylinder with a timer.

As Cinder holstered his weapon, Chen and Lun headed for the front door. Kirby punched in a preset code on the timer panel. Then he stood up, holstered his own gun, and headed for the door after the others.

He turned just before he disappeared from view and stared directly at Nancy.

"It's nice that you're so worried about the poor pandas," he said. "All I can tell you is, if you want to pray for them, you have about a hundred and eighty seconds left to do it."

Then Nancy heard the front door of the house slam closed. Its echo was the only sound to compete with the ticking of the bomb—the bomb that was set to go off in less than three minutes!

Chapter

Sixteen

HEY, YOU GUYS," Joe said, pulling hard against the twine knotted about his wrists, "if anybody has any bright ideas, anything at all, believe me—I'm listening!"

"Crawl for the door," Frank said. "Maybe they didn't lock it."

"No," Mr. Dubchek responded. "I heard the bolt click in."

Joe looked across the room at the bomb. It continued to tick. Every second they were another step closer to doom. One hundred and seventy-five . . . one hundred and seventy-four . . . one hundred and seventy-three . . .

"If we could just stand up," Nancy said, "we

could hop to the door. Or even to the back rooms—anywhere."

"I may be able to get us out of this," Dubchek said. "Just give me a minute."

"Sir," Joe answered. "We don't *have* a minute."

Mr. Dubchek sat upright against the couch and worked his arms up and down, struggling with his bonds. He threaded his fingers between the various strands of twine.

"I watched them while they worked," he said. "They spent more time on your bindings. Just have to get my hand . . . fingers . . . up to the knot . . ."

Ninety-five . . . ninety-four . . . ninety-three . . .

"I can feel it. I've almost got it."

"Better hurry, sir."

"I think he knows that, Joe."

Eighty-seven . . . eighty-six . . .

Then Dubchek's left hand made it out of the first loop. Suddenly his wrists were free from each other by a gap a little wider than a single inch. He pushed himself forward and landed on his face. He dragged himself across the room.

Seventy-nine . . . seventy-eight . . . seventy-seven.

"Mr. Dubchek, what are you doing?" Nancy cried.

"Knife in the desk drawer . . . I use it for a

letter opener . . . think I can get it now . . . get ready . . ."

"We're ready, sir," Joe shouted. "We're ready. Just go, *go!*"

Dubchek flopped forward like a seal. Every painful flip-flop got him a foot and a half closer to his desk.

Sixty-four seconds left.

Mr. Dubchek crashed against his desk. He struggled upward, then fumbled with the drawer handle behind his back.

Fifty-eight seconds left.

"I've got the knife!" he shouted. "I've got it. Just have to turn it, get it in the right position."

"Mr. Dubchek!" Frank shouted. "Are you all right? Can we do *anything?*"

Fifty-one . . . fifty . . . forty-nine . . .

"No, no. I'm all right," Dubchek answered. "Just nicked myself. But I've almost got it . . . almost . . ."

Forty-five . . . forty-four . . .

"Almost through . . . almost . . ."

Forty . . . thirty-nine . . . thirty-eight . . .

"Got it!"

Joe whooped with glee. Frank and Nancy sighed as they saw Mr. Dubchek's arms suddenly break free of the twine.

"Please hurry, sir," Joe urged. "We're almost out of time!"

Thirty-one . . . thirty . . .

"Keep calm, young man," Dubchek answered as he clambered to his feet. "We're going to make it."

"Do you know how to turn the bomb off," Nancy asked. "Can you deactivate it?"

"Not my specialty," Dubchek answered as he bent to work on the twine binding Nancy's ankles.

Twenty-seven . . . twenty-six . . . twenty-five . . .

"Why not just pitch it outside?" Joe asked.

"It's a Grammler. It's got a built-in gyroscope. If they're moved after the countdown begins they go off immediately," Dubchek said.

Twenty-three . . . twenty-two . . .

Joe watched as Dubchek cut through the twine binding Nancy's wrists. He pushed her toward the door. "Go, go—get the door open."

He started on Frank's ankle restraints. "Just keep going. We'll be right behind you!" he called to Nancy.

Twenty . . . nineteen . . . eighteen . . .

As soon as Dubchek cut through the bindings on Frank's ankles, he shoved him upright and started him for the door.

"No time for your wrists—go, go!"

Fifteen . . . fourteen . . .

Dubchek sliced through the twine around Joe's ankles and then jerked him to his feet.

Eleven . . . ten . . .

"Come on, young man—we've got to move!"

Joe and Dubchek crashed against each other moving through the doorway to the front hall.

Eight . . . seven . . .

As they moved through the front door, Joe and Dubchek slammed against each other again. They tangled for only a moment, until Dubchek backed up. Then Joe noticed Dubchek slap the wall near the door with one hand as he pushed Joe forward with the other.

Three . . . two . . .

Joe stumbled onto the front porch of the house. Dubchek came out right behind him. Then, Dubchek took one look at the long flight of stairs and simply grabbed Joe by his shirt collar.

"Jump!" he screamed.

The front wall of the first floor of Mr. Dubchek's home exploded outward. The bulk of the shrapnel narrowly missed Joe and Dubchek as they fell to the ground. Bits of brick and plaster pelted them, but they were laughing as Nancy and Frank ran over to them.

They were alive. For the moment it was enough.

Joe, Frank, and Nancy took Mr. Dubchek a good distance from his burning house in their car.

"Think there's any chance your old friends might have dropped any clues?" Joe asked as he massaged his wrists.

"Doubtful," Dubchek said. "They're professionals."

"Not too professional." Joe laughed, offering his palm to his brother for a high-five. "They keep trying, but we're still alive," he said.

Frank laughed and slapped Joe's hand. "I think we'd better get out of the area. For the moment we have an advantage in the fact that our new playmates have no idea that we got out alive."

Everyone agreed. "This does give us an advantage, although it's only a small one," Mr. Dubchek said as Frank pulled away from the curb.

"Why do you say that, sir?" Nancy asked.

"Because we're still on our own."

"Cinder and Kirby are still CIA agents, aren't they?" Joe asked.

"Yes. Although the agency doesn't know or approve of what they're doing, it may be dangerous for us to assume they're working on their own."

"You think someone higher up might know about the start-up of this plan?" Joe asked.

"I hate to sound melodramatic," Dubchek answered in a sad voice, "but anything is possible. At this point, anyone we approach might be part of the opposition. The same would go for the FBI, the Secret Service . . . even local law enforcement may have been compromised."

"Not everyone in local law enforcement," Nancy said. "Go left, Frank," she said.

Hitting his turn signal, Frank made the first available left and then increased his speed.

Joe was sure he knew where they were headed.

"Oh, come on, Nancy." T-Bone laughed. "You're not serious, are you?"

Joe watched as the big detective studied his and the others' faces. Joe knew the lieutenant would find nothing there to support his theory.

"Lieutenant Vickler," he began, "I know this is a lot to take in, but right now you're the only one we can trust."

"Besides," Frank added, "I'd think with all the property damage that's followed us around town you'd be ready to believe just about anything."

T-Bone Vickler was quiet. Joe could tell the detective was thinking hard. Finally, Vickler said quietly, "All right, let's say I believe all of it—CIA agents, international killers, Vampire squads—"

"They're not really vampires, you know," Joe said. "That's just their code name."

"I know that," the lieutenant answered. "I do pay attention."

"Please, T-Bone," Nancy said, "don't mind Joe. We really have a huge problem here. And you're the only person we *know* we can trust."

"Un-huh," Vickler answered. "And what would you need me to do?"

"I have a plan," Dubchek said. "I've known this man Cinder for a long time. I know Kirby as well. I know what they're like."

"Mr. Dubchek thinks they could be bought off," Nancy said.

"And what about their Chinese partners?" the lieutenant asked.

"I can't be certain about them, of course," Dubchek admitted. "But water seeks its own level. If these men are willing to work with Cinder, they're probably a great deal like him."

"We have to start somewhere," Nancy added.

"As the young lady says, Lieutenant," Dubchek added, "we *do* have to start somewhere. Now, this is my proposal."

Joe noted that Dubchek took a deep breath and then held it for a moment before he began. He had an idea in his head, but he wanted to talk to Frank and Nancy first before he did anything about it. So, he said nothing for the moment and turned his attention to what Dubchek was about to say.

"I talked with these three young people on

the way here. Ms. Drew's father is a prominent attorney. The boys here have a number of government connections. Between them, with you coordinating, I think enough fast money could be found to buy these men off."

"And what would you be doing all this time?" T-Bone asked.

"Me?" Mr. Dubchek answered. "I'll be looking for Cinder, of course. All the money in the world won't help us if we don't have anyone to whom we can give it."

"And how would you manage that?" Joe asked.

"I have a number of connections from the old days. I can put out a message for him. I think I could find him safely."

"Our dad could handle a lot of this," Frank said. "But that would take time that we might not have."

"You're here right now, T-Bone," Nancy said. "You know what's been going on. You don't have to be convinced about any of this. But you have the records and the authority we need to convince other people."

"And," Frank said, "not to be repetitious, but you *are* the only guy we know in this town whom we can trust absolutely."

"Well," Vickler said after a long moment, "I guess I can't pass that up now, can I?"

Mr. Dubchek breathed a sigh of relief. Hearing Vickler's words made everyone feel better instantly. Only Joe remained quiet.

I'm beginning to get a bad feeling about this, he thought to himself. But I can't say anything now. Not until I have more facts.

"I just have one question, though," T-Bone said. "I know it wouldn't be right to let a lot of pandas die, but tell me—why is this *so* important? I mean, aren't these guys sort of right? Don't we want to keep a wedge between China and the Russians?"

"Lieutenant Vickler," Dubchek said, "I'm not a man to worry about the safety of animals over people. I conceived the bamboo operation years ago. Obviously I wasn't worried much about a lot of pandas then, either."

"So, what happened?"

"Lieutenant, things have changed since then. The Chinese are not the same players they were two decades ago. Cinder does not understand the Chinese Communists as I do. They will not endure an insult such as this."

"What makes you so sure of that?" Vickler asked.

"Because the Chinese have been my field of study. They are not a people who will allow their national pride to suffer. They have a staggering atomic arsenal and the will to use it. They've already threatened the United States with nuclear war. Tensions between our two countries are terribly high right now. Charges of human rights abuses, tariff wars, trade wars, the yearly threats from our side to revoke China's Most Favored Nation status—"

"And," Nancy added, "let's not forget about Hong Kong reverting to Chinese rule and all the tension that that's caused. Or think of China laying claim to Taiwan now, and the United States saying no."

"In other words," Frank said, "it'd be bad enough if the Chinese were to get mad at the Soviet Union over this, but if they were to discover that the Russians didn't have anything to do with it—that it was all a U.S. plan . . ."

"Okay, okay," Vickler answered. "I get the idea. How long do we have to get this whole thing moving?"

"No more than twenty-four hours," Dubchek answered. The older man got out of the molded plastic chair. He stretched his arms above his head. "Cinder will listen for reports, wanting to make certain he has eliminated me and these young people. After that he will move and move quickly."

"And if he hears that you're not dead," the lieutenant guessed, "that should slow him—right?"

"I think so," Dubchek answered. "I'm counting on it to slow him down at least long enough for me to find him and get an offer on the table."

"And if it doesn't?" Joe asked. He waited, but it seemed that no one in the room wanted to answer his question.

Chapter

Seventeen

WELL, BOYS, and you, too, Nancy," Fenton Hardy's voice came over the speakerphone, "all I can say is, when you three mix it up, you don't pull any punches."

"We try to make you proud, Dad," Joe answered.

Nancy, the Hardys, and Lieutenant Vickler were sitting in an office tucked away in the rear on an upper floor of the precinct house. Nancy thought of how quickly things had moved in the last few hours.

When T-Bone had told Nancy that he trusted his captain completely, she had agreed that he should inform his superior of the situation. The captain had given them the space as a base of operations and agreed to the situation as long as he was kept posted on the proceedings.

"Thank you, Joseph," Fenton Hardy answered. "Sad to say, my conference hasn't been nearly as exciting for me as it has been for you. But perhaps we'd better get our more immediate problem out of the way."

Nancy had contacted her father and the Hardys had contacted theirs to see if they could set Mr. Dubchek's plan into motion. Both men had jumped in to help. After the initial calls had been made, Dubchek left to try to track down Cinder.

"My contact in the Justice Department, Terrance von Eden, understands the situation," Mr. Hardy said. "He's making the necessary arrangements right now. He'll contact you directly from now on."

"Thanks, Mr. Hardy," Nancy said.

"Just glad to be of help," he answered.

Everyone said their goodbyes and broke the connection. "I'd like to mention something that's been puzzling me before Mr. Dubchek gets back," Nancy said to the others.

"What is it?" Vickler asked.

"This might not be anything, but when we were all tied up at his house," she said, "I noticed that the thugs tied Joe and Frank and myself up with several pieces of rope, but they used only one on Dubchek."

"And?" the lieutenant asked.

"Well, it's an old trick," Nancy said. "It's easier to escape from one long piece of rope than it is from several shorter ones tied together."

"She's right," Frank said. "Houdini made that trick public decades ago."

"He made a comment that he thought they might have treated him more gently because we were younger and stronger," she said, "but to them we were just a bunch of kids and he was an ex–CIA agent. It just didn't add up for me."

"Neither does a guy letting his own house get blown up," Vickler said.

"Maybe it does, though," Joe said, *"if* he's in on it with them."

Nancy stared at Joe. "What are you saying?"

"This has been bothering me. Dubchek and I were the last two out of the house. When we were in the front hall, as he pushed me forward, he slapped the wall. I realize this sounds silly, but he did it as if he were sending a signal of some kind. Or as if he was setting off some kind of trigger."

"This is sounding a little fantastic," Vickler said.

"Maybe," Nancy said. "But perhaps you should have forensics check the wreckage of

Dubchek's home for a triggering device in the vicinity of the front door. And while you're at it, ask them if they know of a type of bomb called a Grammler. It's nothing I've ever heard of."

"Dubchek suggested Cinder and the others could be bribed," Frank said. "Maybe it's not so odd to think that a man might blow up his house if you know he's doing it for a cut of a fifty-million-dollar ransom."

"I must be going nuts," Vickler said with a sigh, "because you're all beginning to make sense."

"Somewhere in there I know there's a compliment," Joe said. "So what do we do now?"

"I say we continue on as planned," Nancy said. "If they're trying to pull something, we don't want them to know we're onto them."

"Sounds like a good idea," Frank said. "Let's just keep our eye on Dubchek and see what he does."

"Makes sense to me," Joe said. "And since food also makes sense to me, I volunteer to go out to get something to eat. Who's in?"

Nancy laughed as Frank and Vickler both pulled money from their wallets and threw it at Joe. Nancy agreed that she could use something as well.

After Joe was on his way, Frank turned to

Nancy. "Do you think we'll have long to wait before things get rolling?" he asked.

"No," Nancy answered. "My father is just waiting to hear from your father's contact at Justice. Once the government gives the authorization, the bankers my father has contacted will be able to start moving cash around pretty fast."

"Even on a weekend?" Vickler asked. "Man, I'm in the wrong business."

Nancy watched sympathetically as the lieutenant stood and stretched his arms out to his sides. Cramped and miserable, he had officially gone off duty almost three hours earlier.

"They don't pay me enough to do *this* stuff."

"Hey," Frank replied. "At least you get paid."

"Nancy—I thought it was just the other one with the bad jokes."

"They're a team, Lieutenant." Nancy laughed. "They cover for each other."

"Yeah?" Vickler said as he lay down on a bench in the corner of the room. "Well, wake me when the rest of the team gets back with our food."

"What if something happens before that?" Frank asked.

"After what I've seen so far," Vickler answered, "all I can ask is—what could happen that you two couldn't handle?"

Nancy smiled but didn't answer.

"Like I said," Vickler added, "just wake me when the food gets here."

Nancy, Frank, Joe, and T-Bone barely had time to begin their meal when the phone rang.

"Got it," Nancy said. She listened for a moment. "I'd like to put you on the speakerphone, Mr. von Eden. Frank, Joe, and Lieutenant Vickler are here with me. Go ahead, sir. Everyone can hear you."

"Frank, Joe," a man's voice came from the speaker, "your father tells me you two need a little spending money."

"That's one way to put it, sir," Joe said.

"Well, rest easy, boys," the Justice official answered. "We've been working out the details on this end as quietly as we can. I understand your Mr. Dubchek's worries about security, but just as your dad felt safe in going to me, I felt safe in taking the matter to the president."

"The president?" Vickler asked with surprise. "The president of the United States?"

"Yes, sir," von Eden answered. "That would be the one. Anyway, since I know our time is tight, let me get right to the point. Nancy, I've already spoken to your father's contacts. They've been able to line up a silent cartel willing to field the accounts we'll need to convince these people that we're on the level."

"How much have they been able to pull together, sir?" Nancy asked.

"The West Coast sources are working on putting together a cash bin of five million, in case you need to show this Cinder actual paper."

Nancy, Frank, Joe, and T-Bone exchanged glances and smiled. "Now we're talking," Joe said.

"And," von Eden said, "that's only the cash front. You'll also have a number of Swiss bank numbers to turn over as well. A simple confirmation phone call on this Cinder's part will let him know there's twenty million more on deposit in the accounts you'll be giving him the codes for."

"Twenty-five million," Joe said. "That's only half what Dubchek thought they'd go for."

"Sorry," von Eden answered, "but with short notice, that's all we've been able to gather assurances for. It is the weekend, you know."

"See?" Vickler said with a smile. "Told you."

"Well, Mr. von Eden," Joe said, "I guess we'll just have to hope twenty-five million is enough."

"It is!"

Nancy turned at the sound of Mr. Dubchek's voice as he entered the office. Before he could speak again, Frank asked, "You found them?"

"Yes," Dubchek answered with excitement.

"I've got them ready to deal, and I'm sure if we can deliver them that much money, quickly, they'll take it and hand over the control disk and those gas samples they have."

"Is that Mr. Dubchek?" von Eden's voice came from the speakerphone.

"Yes, it is," Dubchek answered.

"I'd like to talk to you for a few minutes, sir. This is a serious matter and a great deal of money. The president was hoping I could get a few assurances from you."

"Certainly. If you could give me just a moment."

Nancy's mind returned to her suspicions about Dubchek. "We need to keep this line clear. I gave the number to Cinder so that he could call us when he's ready to arrange the transfer. Is it possible I could call Mr. von Eden back from another line, Lieutenant?"

Vickler directed Mr. Dubchek to another office down the hall where he would be able to talk to von Eden undisturbed. After getting the Justice man's phone number, Dubchek hung up and then headed immediately for the other office.

"So," Nancy said, "who thinks he's on our side?"

"He comes back and *knows* how much these guys can be bribed with," Joe said. "I think we're getting played for saps."

"I think you're right, too," Frank said. "But we can't just grab Dubchek. Cinder and the others would still be free to do whatever they wanted. Including setting three nuclear powers at one anothers' throats."

"Hold on, everyone," Vickler said. "We're not supposed to convict people without evidence. But we are allowed a certain amount of latitude when it comes to following our instincts. And my instincts tell me you three are right about this—which is bad."

"Why?" Nancy asked.

"Because we're going to have to play along with him until he makes his move," Vickler said. "It could be a dangerous game."

Nancy answered with a smile, "Perhaps we can do something to even the odds a little."

Nancy pressed the speaker function before the first ring had finished. Nancy and the Hardys sat to the left of the desk with the phone. Dubchek, Lieutenant Vickler, and the two Treasury agents who had brought the cash sat in front of it and to the right.

"Hello, Carl," Cinder's voice rang through the room. "I hope you have everything ready."

"We're ready, pal," Joe snapped. "You just better live up to your end of the bargain."

"Young Mr. Hardy, so glad to hear you so fit and hale."

"No thanks to you, pal," Joe retorted.

"Gentlemen," Cinder said, "if this is an attempt to stall this call so it can be traced, it will do you no good. We are speaking to you from a cell phone. Furthermore, we are in constant motion and the signal is being routed through a floating pick-up station off the coast."

"I told them to expect as much," Mr. Dubchek said. "I believe everyone is aware of with whom they're dealing."

"Good," Cinder said. "If we're obeyed, then we'll be rich and the bears will be saved. You will be poorer, but the world will work the way you wish it to, and more important, no one will have been hurt."

"Just tell us what to do," Joe said.

"Ah, the impatience of youth. Very well, Mr. Hardy, this is what you need to do. First, tell me how much money you have arranged."

"Twenty-five million," Mr. Dubchek answered. "Five million in cash, twenty in Swiss deposits. They can be verified with a phone call—"

"I still understand international finance, Carl," Cinder's voice shot back. After a pause, he spoke again. "Very well, my associates and I agree that this will suffice. That being the case, this is what else you need to do. You will drive in a car that will be provided. Don't bother to bring tracking devices with you. The car has been set up to jam them."

"Magnets," one of the Treasury agents whispered.

"Probably," Mr. Dubchek whispered back.

"If you tamper with this, we'll know," Cinder continued. "There is nothing for you to memorize or write down. You will find a cell phone inside the car. You will receive your instructions by phone as you bring the money to us."

"And who makes this delivery?" Vickler asked.

"Why, like all circles, this one should end where it began. Carl—the bamboo operation was your idea. Since you conceived it, you shall end it."

"It's too much money," protested one of the Treasury agents. "Mr. Dubchek wouldn't even be able to carry all the cases himself."

"Oh, don't worry." Cinder's voice curled out of the speaker like a viper. "We wouldn't let Carl make the trip by himself."

"Good," Vickler said. "We'll be sending—"

"You," Cinder snapped, "will shut up and do as you're told."

Nancy and the others remained quiet, waiting for the rogue CIA agent's next commands. "As I was saying, the good lawyer is certainly too old to make such a trip by himself. No, he'll have to have company. Someone to help with the driving, to look for signs, to keep him awake with friendly chatter."

"Okay," Joe said. "Spill it. Who goes?"

"You do, along with your brother and the lovely Ms. Drew. And if anyone else comes along . . . if any attempt is made to follow you, if any of our instructions aren't followed to the letter, we'll kill you all and immediately return to our original plan. Do you understand?"

"Yes," Nancy answered. "We get the idea. Just tell us when we start."

"Why, Ms. Drew, your car has been in front of the police station for the last ten minutes. The keys are in an envelope at the front desk. You start *right now.*"

Chapter

Eighteen

HERE IT IS," Frank said. He pointed through the early-evening twilight at a late-model car. The car was parked at the curb in a spot reserved for police vehicles only.

"They're lucky they didn't get a ticket," Joe said. He slid one of the suitcases containing the five-million-dollar ransom into the trunk of the car.

"Wouldn't that be our kind of luck," he added, handing the next case to his brother. "The world ends in nuclear fire because the bad guys' car got towed."

"Please," Mr. Dubchek said, "let's not even joke about this not turning out all right."

"You got it, sir," Joe answered.

As Frank packed the last of the money cases, Nancy said, "It *is* chilly out here. I'm glad T-Bone was able to dig up these sweatshirts for us."

"LAPD sweatshirts," Frank said as he closed the car's trunk. "They'll make great souvenirs."

"Yeah," Joe added grimly. "If we live long enough to show them to anyone."

"So," Nancy asked, "who's driving?"

"If you youngsters wouldn't mind," Dubchek said, "I'd like to just sit in the backseat."

Frank looked over at Joe and nodded. "I don't see why that would be a problem," Nancy said. "Make yourself comfortable and we'll get moving."

"I've got the keys," Frank said. "Want me to start us out?"

Nancy and Joe agreed readily. As Nancy slid into the front seat, Frank stood outside the driver's door. Joe stood by the rear door, waiting for Dubchek to finish getting inside. He heard Lieutenant Vickler call out, "Hey, wait up."

"What's wrong, T-Bone?" Joe asked.

"Nothing," Vickler answered. "The Treasury boys thought you might want something to drink."

This is it, Frank thought. When we talked to

T-Bone earlier, he said he'd work out something with the Treasury men to help us out. But it was such short notice—what could they have come up with?

Vickler held up a six pack of bottled sodas and said, "Of course, if you don't want them . . ."

"Hand them over, T-Bone," Joe said with a smile and knowing wink. "And tell the G-men thanks."

Frank knew Dubchek couldn't see him and gave Vickler a quick nod. The officer nodded back to him, then continued his part of the charade.

"Sure," he answered as he took one of the bottles and tossed it to Joe. "Here—catch."

Joe stuck out his arm but missed the bottle, allowing it to smash against the roof of the car. Instantly Dubchek jumped out through the side door and shouted, "What was that? What happened?"

"Relax," Joe said easily. "It was just T-Bone here throwing like a girl—"

"You mean it was you catching like a girl," the lieutenant responded.

"Oh, boys," Nancy said in a singsong voice, "do you both want to get smacked in the head by a girl?"

"No, ma'am," Vickler answered as he passed

the remaining bottles to Joe. "That wouldn't be any fun at all."

Frank watched Dubchek. Dubchek ignored everyone else as he studied the car roof. Joe held up the cardboard container with the five remaining bottles. "Nothing to worry about. Just a little fruit juice and sparkling water," he said.

Dubchek smiled weakly, then reentered the car. Joe got in and slammed the door.

"Here's the phone, just as they said." Nancy slid into the front seat. "It's got a note attached."

"What is it?" Frank asked. "A number for us to call?"

"You guessed it," Nancy answered. She punched in the number. Frank gunned the engine while they waited for the line to connect.

The late-night street was silent, except for the drip-drip of soda from the roof of the car to the street. That, and the sound of the all-too-rapid beating of their hearts.

When Frank called the number on the note he got a recorded message directing him to take Route 101 north out of Los Angeles. Defiantly, Cinder had even given the address of the hotel where the answering machine had been set up—along with the room number. Frank listened as the tape instructed him to call the police and give them that information freely.

Then the tape had given Frank a tense warning "That will be your last contact with the police," Cinder's voice said. "We'll be watching your progress. We'll call you from time to time to see if you're using the phone. If we find the line is busy, we will go back to the plan. If any of our observers spot that you are being followed, we will go back to the plan. If you've brought another phone with you, it won't work. Only the phone connected to the car's internal antenna can foil the car's trace baffler. Do anything that varies from our instructions and we will go back to the plan."

Frank continued to drive. He didn't try to disregard Cinder's instructions. That's what the guy expects, Frank thought. As Dad always says, never do what they expect.

It was already growing dark when the foursome left Los Angeles. Now the evening sky was pitch-black. Cinder had sent Frank and the others up the California Coast Road. It was a scenic route during the daytime, one filled with panoramic views of the Pacific Ocean and beautiful forestlands. At night, however, it became a dark and dangerous road, badly lit and filled with sharp curves.

"Cinder went out of his way to make sure no one was following us," Joe said with a yawn.

"Well, I guess turning traitor and extortionist makes some guys overly paranoid," Frank answered.

Frank spoke quietly, as did Joe. He had driven so long he had to stop for gas—after Cinder had phoned him to tell him the gas tank was almost empty. After Frank had taken off again, Nancy settled in to take a nap.

"Still scares me, though," Joe said, "how Cinder knew when we were almost out of gas."

"Well," Frank offered, "he did say he had people watching us."

"Must be a lot of them," Joe responded. "The way he always seems to know where we are, always calling when he wants us to pull off or double around or anything."

"He *is* a CIA agent," Frank reminded his brother. He wondered if they were really being watched from the outside.

Could Dubchek be signaling Cinder? Frank thought. It would explain a lot.

Frank did not want Dubchek to grow suspicious. "CIA agents are supposed to be good at this sort of thing," he said to his brother.

"Yeah, maybe," Joe answered. "I don't have to like it, though."

The phone rang again. Joe answered it and put the call on speaker. "City Morgue—you stab 'em, we slab 'em. What can we do for you?"

"Your humor leaves something to be desired, Mr. Hardy."

"Funny, that's just what my teachers always say. You don't have a part-time job in the education field, do you, Cinder?"

"If you're asking me if I'd like to teach you a lesson, Mr. Hardy, let me just say that perhaps it would be best for you if we put off this discussion for a while. I have some directions for your brother."

"What now, Cinder?" Frank asked.

"Now, now, Mr. Hardy," the CIA agent answered. "Not so testy. Your travels will be at an end soon. At least, your travels by automobile."

"Great—what's next? We transfer to hot-air balloon?"

"What's that?" Mr. Dubchek asked. He sounded confused. "What's he talking about?"

"I think he was just joking," Joe explained.

At the same time, Cinder told Frank, "You should have just passed the sign for Refugio Pass, correct?"

"You should know," Frank answered.

"Good. You'll see a turnoff on your left a few miles up the road. It will say Dagon Beach. Make that turn."

Frank snapped on the overhead light. He

referred quickly to the map on the dashboard, which had been folded open to display the stretch of road they were on. He checked the rectangle again, then said into the phone, "Dagon Beach? I don't have anything like that on my map."

"Dagon Beach," Mr. Dubchek muttered. He repeated the name several times, then said suddenly, "Do as he says, Frank. I know where we're going."

"I thought you would, Carl," Cinder said with a chuckle. "That means you know where to go."

Mr. Dubchek nodded repeatedly. "I should have known, I should have known," he whispered.

If you're lying to us, Dubchek, Frank thought, you're doing a really good job. All I can say is, if you *are* a traitor, you should have been an actor.

Frank slowed the car as he came to an extremely sharp turn around a blind hillside. Then, on the other side of the hill, he suddenly spotted the sign for Dagon Beach. Slowing the car even more, he made the turn off the main road as Cinder had instructed.

As he drove down the seemingly new but unused road, he commented, "That was an awfully small sign back there. If you hadn't cued me I'd never have seen it."

"That's because people aren't supposed to see it, Mr. Hardy," Cinder answered. "Why don't you ask your friend Carl to explain. And please, let's leave the phone connection open from here on in. Thank you, Mr. Hardy. I'll be seeing you again shortly."

"Mr. Dubchek," Frank asked as he set the phone on the seat next to him, leaving it switched on as Cinder had ordered, "what did he mean? Cinder just told me that people aren't supposed to be able to find this Dagon Beach."

"No," Dubchek answered. "No, they're not."

"Why not?" Joe asked. "Is it a private beach?"

"In a manner of speaking," Dubchek answered. "It is possibly one of the most private beaches in the world. Dagon Beach is a staging area. One of the agency's older ones. Maybe even abandoned by now. I hadn't thought about it for years."

Frank slowed the car as the road suddenly grew rougher. He swerved to miss one large pothole, throwing Nancy forward.

"Nice driving, Hardy," Nancy said as she snapped awake. "Trying out for the Indianapolis Five-hundred?"

"Not tonight," Frank answered. "But if you really think I'm good enough, I'll consider it."

189

Nancy looked from Frank to Joe and then back again. "I don't know which one of you makes the worst jokes. But, please, don't try to help me figure it out now. Just tell me when we get close to wherever it is we're going."

"Well, then," Frank responded, "consider this your wake-up call, Ms. Drew."

"We're here?"

"We're close," Dubchek said. "If I remember the area correctly—very close. When the agency sent missions into the Pacific region and down into Latin America, back in the early seventies, this was the launch area."

"So, what kind of place is it?" Nancy asked. "Just a beach? Or does it have a dock? Or is it a complete complex of some kind?"

"You'll be able to see for yourself any moment now," Dubchek answered.

Before anyone could question Mr. Dubchek further, Cinder's voice called from the phone. Nancy answered it.

"What was that? We couldn't hear you."

"I was cautioning you to slow down—you're coming up to the end of the road rapidly."

Frank pumped the brakes lightly, then hit them harder only a second later as a large metal gate suddenly appeared across the road.

As Frank stopped the car, Nancy asked, "There's a gate across the road, Cinder. What do we do now?"

"Now," the agent answered, "you get out of the car and you walk. Carl can lead you. I'm certain he remembers the way."

Frank cut the engine and pocketed the keys. Hitting the switch on the side of the dashboard that opened the trunk, he said, "Okay, everybody, now we know what he meant when he said we were finished traveling by car."

As everyone exited the vehicle, Joe asked, "What about it, Mr. Dubchek? Do you know where we're supposed to go?"

"Yes," Dubchek answered. "There's only one place to go." Pointing off into the dark distance, he said, "We go down over these dunes to the beach. After a while we'll come to a cove. There's a cave in the back of it. That's where they are."

"Well," Frank said, pulling one of the money cases out of the trunk, "at least now we know why we found these flashlights in the trunk."

"Fine," Nancy said. "Pass them out and let's get this over with."

Within seconds all of the suitcases were out of the trunk. With Dubchek and Nancy taking the lead and Frank following, Joe reached up to shut the trunk lid.

"Go ahead," he told the others. "I'm right behind you."

Then Joe slammed the trunk and took a last look at the dried residue on the roof of the car from the bottle he and T-Bone had so carefully broken back in Los Angeles. From the top of the dune, Frank looked down at Joe. He knew what his brother was thinking.

Frank turned his eyes toward the sky. When he saw nothing, he thought, And here's another fine mess we've gotten ourselves into.

Chapter

Nineteen

"HEY," NANCY SHOUTED. "Look—back here. Here it is."

The cave entrance was barely wide enough to admit one of them at a time. So narrow was the opening that not even Nancy could enter carrying her suitcase. The money cases would have to be handed in one at a time.

"Mr. Dubchek," Joe suggested, "why don't you head in first. At least you've been here before. Then you help Nancy inside. Frank and I will pass the bags in after that."

Nancy began to protest the implication that she would need help, but Joe gave her a look that let her know he was up to something. She didn't know what he could be doing, but she had been in desperate situations with the Hardys often enough to know that she had to trust him—just as he would have trusted her if the situation had been reversed.

Nancy pulled the bags in one at a time as Frank and Joe passed them through the narrow entrance. Then Frank came through just before the last case.

"Here," he said to Dubchek, "let me help you with the money. Joe and Nancy can get the last one through without us."

Nancy watched Frank as he purposely positioned himself between her and Dubchek.

He's blocking Dubchek's field of vision, she realized. What's he up to?

"Here you go, but don't worry," Joe called to Nancy. "This is an easy one. It's the *lightest* one."

Nancy caught the tone in Joe's voice. She knew he was giving her a clue about something. But what, she wondered? Then, as her hands began to pull the suitcase through the entrance, she realized what Joe had been trying to warn her about.

The suitcase was empty!

As Joe came through the entrance behind the case, Nancy stared at him. She tried to figure out what had happened to the money that should have been inside the now empty case.

Silently, Joe mouthed two words: Trust me.

Then Dubchek was standing next to Nancy again. Nancy decided it would be best to trust Joe as he had asked.

"Okay," she said. "Let's get going."

As they moved forward, she, Frank, and Joe played their lights across the ceiling and walls of the cave. She could see spots where the space had been enlarged; the floor also appeared to be unnaturally level.

After a few minutes Nancy and the others reached a spot where the cavern split off into three different tunnels.

"Okay, Mr. Dubchek," she asked. "Which way do we go now?"

Nancy watched as Dubchek reviewed the different passageways for a moment. He finally answered, gesturing to the right, "This way. The docks are this way."

"Docks, sir?" Joe asked. "Getting a little like James Bond here, aren't we?"

"I suppose you could look at it that way, son," Dubchek answered. "But remember, the agency gets itself involved in a lot of things the government has to be able to deny knowledge of. It's hard to outfit an invasion force without anyone's knowing if you do it out in the open."

"So, Mr. Dubchek," Nancy asked, "you're telling us that there's an underground docking facility in here—and that as soon as we turn over this money, Cinder and his people are going to have direct access to the open sea?"

"Yes," Dubchek said. "I'm afraid they've planned this rather well."

Then as Nancy, Frank, Joe, and Dubchek rounded the next corner, light was visible ahead of them. As Nancy and the others slowed involuntarily, a voice called out to them from above.

"Please, this is no time for dawdling."

"Cinder," Nancy called out. "Where are you?"

"Somewhere I can watch you quite easily. Now walk forward into the light."

As the drop team moved toward the illumination before them, the cavern began to open up. After only a few more steps Nancy, Frank and Joe found themselves in a wide expanse supported by a network of steel girders. Enough docking bays ran along the far wall to accommodate a score of medium-size crafts. In the first slip, Nancy saw a waiting speedboat with Kirby at its wheel.

"That's far enough."

Nancy realized that Cinder's voice was coming from a speaker mounted on the ceiling of the cavern. As they stopped, Nancy and Frank set their suitcases down in front of them. Nancy noted that Joe did the same with the one he was carrying, the empty one, but that he then stepped in front of it.

At the same time she saw Lun and Chen as they made their way forward out of the shadows. Both were armed with automatic weapons. Again, Cinder's voice sounded from overhead.

"Ms. Drew, and the brothers Hardy . . . so good to see you all again."

"That's hard to believe," Frank said. "Especially since the last time you saw us, you tried to kill us with a bomb."

As Lun moved forward toward the money case in front of Nancy, Joe said, "Oh, come on, Frank. I mean, it's not like we were actually in any danger then. Although we have to give Dubchek credit, he sure did go all out to make it exciting for us."

As Lun made a move to pass Joe, Joe stepped into the thug's path, saying, "Hey, come on, what's the hurry? You've got us, you've got the money. You're in charge. Don't you want to hear how we figured out that Dubchek is one of you?"

Mr. Dubchek turned and stared at Joe. "I don't know what you're talking about, young man," he sputtered.

"Playing it all the way to the end?" Nancy asked.

As Dubchek moved his hands helplessly in front of him, Nancy turned as Cinder's voice sounded again, this time from the area of the docks.

"Oh, bravo, Mr. Hardy. Bravo."

Clapping his hands together as if applauding a favorite singer, Cinder moved toward the drop team. "Mr. Lun, give them a moment. Mr. Hardy is right. I must hear this," he said.

"So—how did the dear lawyer give himself away? Tell us, please," Cinder said.

"You made a lot of mistakes," Nancy told Cinder as Dubchek moved to join Lun and Chen. "But I guess the worst was underestimating us. Things like trying to make us believe we were being watched no matter where we were. My guess is Dubchek has a signal device on him that he would set off whenever it was time for you to call. He sees a landmark, buzzes you, you say 'Oh, you just reached so-and-so.' Right?"

"I'll give you that one," Cinder said. "Earn the rest."

"Easy," Nancy answered. "One would be Dubchek's line about how easy it would be to turn you from idealists into thieves. We've dealt with both types before, and neither changes so easily. That was when we were sure this had to be about money and was from the beginning."

"Of course, there were other things," Joe added. "When Dubchek and I escaped from his house, I noticed him slap the wall as we went through the front door. I told the LAPD to check for a triggering device in the rubble near the door. They found the remains of one, which made a lot more sense than what Dubchek called the Grammler."

Nancy paused. "There is no such bomb," Nancy added. "We checked."

"They were just kids," Dubchek sputtered as Cinder came forward out of the shadows. Nancy noted the traveling mike in his hand.

"That's why we decided to use them," Dubchek shouted as he ran toward Cinder. "Remember? They fit the plan perfectly."

"And what could that plan have been?" Nancy asked. "Let me guess. You present yourselves as nasty master criminals out to shove the world to the brink of nuclear war by threatening cute little pandas. You picked the U.N. environmental conference because you expected everyone there to be a sucker and easily manipulated."

Nancy put her hands to her face. "Nuclear war, hurting animals—oh my!" she said in a mock-frightened voice.

"That was why you had your very public theft of the bamboo," Frank added. "And the clumsy burning of the warehouse. And even killing your own men. You wanted people out there to put two and two together easily so they could pat themselves on the back for figuring out what was going on."

"But you never expected Anthony Green to actually fall in love with Bess," Nancy said harshly. "Did you?"

"No," Cinder said. He chuckled. "That did throw a wrench into things. But only for a moment. Anthony Green, Ms. Marvin, and yourself were easily eliminated from the equation. It was only when you resurfaced that we decided you would make just as good a patsy as anyone. Better than many."

Cinder walked back and forth in front of Nancy and the others. He kept his weapon at waist level, always pointed at either her or one of the Hardys as he continued.

"A little research on you three made you sound perfect for our needs," Cinder admitted. "A believable trio of witnesses to our horrid deeds, kids with contacts in high places who could work the available money pool as easily as anyone else. And quickly, too, before calmer heads could prevail."

Cinder stroked his chin with his free hand as he said, "People are so willing to believe the CIA capable of anything. We were certain a bunch of little kiddies would eat up our be-mean-to-the-pandas story."

"But that story was a fake, too, wasn't it?" Nancy demanded. "There never was a kill-the-pandas plan—was there?"

"What makes you so certain?" Cinder asked.

"Because," Joe said, "Dubchek here held up a computer disk and told us he hadn't looked at it since 1978. There *were* no three-and-a-quarter-inch disks in 1978."

"And let's go back to the warehouse fire while we're at it," Frank said. "The car from the hotel shooting—CIA agents would know that any good forensics team would be able to find all of the clues easily. I expect you even left the gun from the shooting in the backseat."

"In the trunk, actually," Cinder admitted. "But congratulations, anyway."

"So," Joe asked, nodding toward Lun and Chen, "are these guys really Chinese agents? Or is that just part of the con?"

"Oh, no, Mr. Hardy," Cinder answered. "Mr. Lun and Mr. Chen are indeed members of the Gaun Cee Qui. But they are members as weary of their government's inability to maintain a single course of action as are Mr. Kirby, the good lawyer, and myself."

"So," Nancy said, "you concocted this plan together and—"

"No, no," Cinder interrupted Nancy. "The plan was all Dubchek's. And the funny thing is, not only didn't the CIA invent the bamboo gas, the Red Chinese did."

"It's true," Chen said, his face broken by a

wide smile. "The pandas stood in the way of farm expansion. They could have easily been sacrificed to the needs of the Communist ideal."

"Yes," Lun continued, "but when it was seen what monies there were to be made from the West by keeping them alive, the plan was shelved. But as you can see, not entirely forgotten."

"All well and good," Cinder said as he looked at his watch. "But time is growing short. I think the moment has arrived for us to collect our booty and retire to our launch."

Nancy watched as Lun moved forward once more and grabbed the suitcase in front of Frank. She noted that Lun was careful to stay out of their reach and also out of his fellow agents' lines of fire. The thug pulled the case back smoothly and then went for the one in front of Nancy. As he did, Joe continued to stand his ground in front of his suitcase.

Oh, Joe, Nancy wondered, what did you do with the money?

Before she could think of an answer, Cinder cocked his weapon and aimed it directly at Joe.

"Now, now, children," he said. "No more playtime. Let's have that last bag."

"Wait," Joe said. "Don't you want to know how we—"

"No," Cinder snapped. "I suddenly get the

distinct impression that you're stalling us. Move away from the bag."

Lun and Chen brought their weapons up, fingers on the triggers. As Dubchek started for the docked speedboat with one of the money cases, Joe stepped away from the last suitcase. Lun waved his weapon back and forth from Nancy and Frank to Joe, forcing them to step back even farther. Then he grabbed the last case, only to make a startling discovery.

"It's *empty!*"

"What?" Cinder shouted.

"What are you talking about?" Dubchek screamed and dropped the bag in his hand. He ran back toward the others and shouted, "I saw them. I saw them fill the bags. I watched them get loaded into the trunk. It has to be full. It *has* to be!"

Lun popped open the last suitcase.

"Does it *look* full, old man?" he sneered.

"I doubt this is the good lawyer's doing." Cinder said. He aimed his weapon at Joe's chest and said, "You're the one who's been doing the most stalling. Where's my money?"

"Cinder," Joe asked, "did you ever hear the story of Hansel and Gretel?"

"You're not going to tell me you've been leaving a million-dollar breadcrumb trail from Los Angeles to here, are you?"

"No, we didn't have to do that," Joe answered. "Back in L.A., Lieutenant Vickler and I covered the car you left us with a chemical that shows up only under ultraviolet light."

"That's impossible!" Dubchek snapped. "I was with them every minute," Dubchek told Cinder. "There was no chance for them to, to . . ." Then Dubchek remembered the soft drink bottle that had smashed against the roof.

"Oh my!" Dubchek said as he grabbed Cinder's jacket. "We were followed—we *were* followed!"

Cinder slapped Dubchek and stepped past the older man, his gun leveled at Joe.

"Where's my money, you punk!"

"The Treasury agents who delivered the money, it was their plan," Joe said. "We mark the car, and then they have it followed by a squad of Black Bugs."

They all recognized the nickname for the Air Force's silent running surveillance helicopters.

"He's got to be telling the truth," Dubchek cried. "My goodness, Vandenberg Air Force Base is just up the road."

"I don't care!" Cinder growled as he stepped forward and smacked Joe across the face. "I don't care about anything except the money!"

Nancy watched as Cinder pointed his weapon directly at Joe. She wanted to do something to help, but Lun and Chen had their guns on her and Frank.

There's nothing I can do, she thought. She stared at Cinder. Sweat rolled off the agent's forehead. "What did you do with my money?" he screamed, a wild look in his eyes.

"I used it to mark a trail from the car to the cave," Joe answered. "With Dubchek leading the way, he never saw a thing. It's funny—but I thought the cavalry would've been here by now."

Just then a noise started to grow from a point near where they had entered the cavern.

"Hey," Nancy said with hope. "Maybe that's them now."

She watched as panic flashed across each of the agents' faces. Dubchek grabbed one of the money cases and ran for the boat. Chen and Lun grabbed the other, both pulling in different directions. As Cinder turned his head for a moment, distracted by his co-conspirators, Joe threw himself sideways, knocking the man's legs out from under him.

With every second, the sound of heavy boots grew louder and louder. Nancy raced back toward the entrance.

"This way," she shouted.

She turned back and looked toward the docks just in time to see Kirby start the speedboat. He moved it out of its slip as fast as he could, leaving before any of his co-conspirators could get to it.

"No!" Dubchek screamed. "Wait for us."

Nancy saw Chen take aim at the boat and fire. His shot cut Kirby down and left the speedboat to crash into the dock. Seconds later the Treasury assault team reached the illuminated area of the cavern and poured in past Nancy.

"Watch out," she said. "There are three of them left, and they're all armed!"

As the agents fanned out, officers shouting orders, guns being brought to the ready, Cinder scrambled to his feet.

"You!" he shouted at Joe. "It's your fault. You're the one who stalled us—who brought everything down." The agent lifted and aimed his weapon.

"Well, punk," he said, "thanks for the good time."

Then Nancy watched helplessly as Cinder fired three bullets from his weapon, all striking Joe full in the chest!

Chapter

Twenty

SO THEN WHAT HAPPENED?" Bess asked.

"What happened then?" Joe said. "That's when the creep shot me!"

Joe smiled. He could tell from the way Bess was looking at him that she was wondering if his last comment had been another joke.

"You don't look very shot," she said with a frown.

Joe nodded and pulled up the front of the loose sweater he was wearing. As he did, he grimaced with pain, but eventually he revealed the bandages running around his body.

"But, Joe," Bess protested, "you said those people had automatics. You don't get bandaged

207

up after being shot by an automatic weapon. Even I know that."

"Well," T-Bone admitted, "I have to confess that it's my fault the human joke machine is still with us."

"And we all thank you," Frank said.

"You see, Bess," Joe said, "by the time we had gotten the whole ball rolling with the Treasury Department, we were certain that Mr. Dubchek was double-crossing us. T-Bone outfitted us all with bulletproof vests. To cover them, he gave us all LAPD sweatshirts."

"We used the excuse that it gets cold here at night," Nancy added. "Since Mr. Dubchek already had a jacket, he didn't catch on."

"Almost wasn't enough, though," Joe admitted. "That cannon Cinder shot me with really packed a wallop. I can still feel it."

"What you're feeling is two cracked ribs," Joe's doctor said. "Personally, I think you should still be in bed."

"No way, sir," Joe answered. "We Hardys have to be ready for action and adventure at a moment's notice. I could miss all kinds of thrills lying around here all day."

"Tell me about it," Bess said. "You three solved the whole case without me."

"You did have a good excuse for not being with us," Nancy said with sympathy.

"Yeah," Joe added, "she knocked herself silly tripping over a table."

"Watch it, Joe," Bess snapped.

Joe ignored Bess and turned to his brother.

"Nice girl . . . big feet, though."

Joe laughed as he felt Bess's pillow bounce off the back of his head.

"Truce," he shouted. "I surrender."

"You don't have to be so mean," Bess answered.

"Aw, I was just kidding," Joe admitted. "Really, I was just trying to cheer you up. Are you okay now?"

"Yes," Bess answered. "I talked to my mom for a long time last night. She helped me straighten everything out. But thanks for caring."

"Your mom's here?" Nancy asked.

"She and Dad got here last night," Bess explained. "Which you would have known if you all weren't off having fun."

"Fun she calls it." Joe rubbed his aching ribs lightly. "You're twisted."

"If I could break in for a second," the doctor interrupted. "I'd just like to say, Mr. Hardy, that you may leave whenever you like."

"What about Bess?" Nancy asked. "When will she be able to leave?"

"Her discharge is up to me," the doctor

answered with a smile. "And I'm happy to report that she can leave any time she's feeling up to it."

Crossing the room to Bess's side, the doctor asked, "What do you say, Ms. Marvin, have you had enough hospital food to last you for a while?"

"A long while," Bess answered.

"Well," the doctor said, "your father's taken care of all the paperwork. All you have to do is buzz the nurse when you're ready to leave. She'll check out your valuables from the hospital safe and bring you your clothes."

Bess said, "You know, I've heard the whole story now, and I have to ask . . . what made Cinder and the others think they could get away with such a convoluted plan?"

"I've seen a lot of criminals," Vickler said, "and my best guess is, they knew about the old Chinese plan to kill off the pandas. It was something they figured they could make something out of. Crooks are all the same—give 'em some little advantage, and they'll twist it out of all proportion."

"And," Nancy added, "Cinder himself said that as soon as anyone says something like the evil CIA did this or that, everyone is always prepared to buy it immediately."

"That's true," Frank said. "I also think they were counting on the complicated layers of their deception keeping the authorities busy so that by the time anyone figured things out they would be on their boat with their money and far away."

"Speaking of money," Bess asked, "what about all that cash you threw all over the ground? Did the government find it all?"

"Oh, yeah," Joe answered. He had to laugh at the memory, even though it hurt to do so. "The Department of the Treasury doesn't lose a million dollars easily. Besides, I tossed it out in the little bundles it came wrapped in."

"Thank you for letting me listen to your incredible story," the doctor said, "but I'd better excuse myself. Those of us without such exciting lives still have things we have to do."

"What about you?" Joe asked his brother as the doctor left. "You started this case telling me about how seniors have to think about the future and all. How about it? Have you decided what you want to do with the rest of your life?"

"Oh, I don't know," Frank answered. "I guess I could put up with poking around a few more mysteries with you."

"Well, that's sweet to hear," Vickler said. "But I'd better get going." Pointing to Joe, he added, "I just wanted to make sure Joe was okay and all. I did get kind of attached to him."

"Yeah," Joe answered, "I love you, too, T-Bone."

The lieutenant shook hands with everyone, then headed for the door. He stopped just before he passed into the hallway. He turned and said, "I just have to ask this one last thing. I made some calls when this all started, and I checked up on you all. People from your hometowns, I mean law enforcement people, not the barber or grocer, they all swore that this kind of stuff happens to you all the time."

"Well," Joe said, patting his broken ribs gently, "we're usually not this sloppy. But, yeah, more so than to the rest of the world, I guess."

"Amazing," T-Bone said, shaking his head. "Simply amazing."

"It's not that amazing," Bess answered. A grin filled with mischief spread across her face as she added, "After all, Lieutenant, this is Nancy Drew—"

"Don't you say it," Nancy threatened, knowing where her friend was headed.

"Teen sleuth—"

"I'm warning you . . ."

"Girl detective—"

"That did it!" Nancy said.

Nancy grabbed playfully for her friend as Bess rolled off the other side of the bed. Laughing, she added, "And her two dimwitted assistants, the Hardy Boys."

"Dimwitted?" Joe said.

"Assistants?" Frank asked.

As Nancy backed Bess into a corner of the room, Joe and Frank followed, saying in unison, "Tickle torture!"

"Lieutenant!" Bess shouted, giggling between every word, "You have to save me!"

T-Bone walked down the hall laughing. He watched with amusement as nurses headed for Bess's room to see what all the screaming was about.

THE HARDY BOYS CASEFILES

"Well, we could grind our enemies into powder with a sledgehammer, but gosh, we did that last night."   - Xander

BUFFY

THE VAMPIRE

SLAYER™

As long as there have been vampires, there has been the Slayer. One girl in all the world, to find them where they gather and to stop the spread of their evil and the swell of their numbers.

#1 THE HARVEST
A Novelization by Richie Tankersley Cusick
Based on the teleplays by Joss Whedon

#2 HALLOWEEN RAIN
By Christopher Golden and Nancy Holder

#3 COYOTE MOON
By John Vornholt

#4 NIGHT OF THE LIVING RERUN
By Arthur Byron Cover

All new adventures
based on the hit TV series created by Joss Whedon

From Archway Paperbacks
Published by Pocket Books   1399-03